PAUL ZINDEL

The Amazing and Death-Defying Diary of Eugene Dingman

BANTAM BOOKS
NEW YORK · TORONTO · LONDON · SYDNEY · AUCKLAND

RL 6, IL age 12 and up

*This edition contains the complete text
of the original hardcover edition.*
NOT ONE WORD HAS BEEN OMITTED.

THE AMAZING AND DEATH-DEFYING DIARY OF EUGENE DINGMAN

A Bantam Book / published by arrangement with Harper & Row

*PRINTING HISTORY
Harper & Row edition published October 1987
Bantam edition / March 1989*

*The Starfire logo is a registered trademark of Bantam Books, a division of Bantam
Doubleday Dell Publishing Group, Inc. Registered in U.S. Patent and Trademark Office
and elsewhere.*

ISBN 0-553-27768-5

Published simultaneously in the United States and Canada

*Bantam Books are published by Bantam Books, a division of Bantam Doubleday Dell
Publishing Group, Inc. Its trademark, consisting of the words "Bantam Books" and the
portrayal of a rooster, is Registered in U.S. Patent and Trademark Office and in other
countries. Marca Registrada. Bantam Books, 1540 Broadway, New York, New York
10036.*

PRINTED IN THE UNITED STATES OF AMERICA

OPM   14 13 12 11 10 9 8 7

The Amazing and
Death-Defying Diary
of Eugene Dingman

Things I will never forget about today are:

1) I threw a spoon at my mother's left leg when she was talking about Mr. Mayo.

2) Pearl Buck and Peter Lorre were born, both of whom are dead now.

3) I read in my *History of the World* book that beards were frowned upon in Paris in the fourteenth century because it was felt they made men look like wolves.

4) I heard my sister, Penelope, crying in her room.

5) It is my fifteenth birthday, and I decided to begin writing my first, extremely personal, diary.

11:17 P.M.

I'm upset about throwing the spoon at my mother's leg. I very much need to talk to someone, to be completely honest and try to come to terms with what's going on inside of me. I don't have that many friends at the moment. Calvin Kennedy is the best one. It's probably just as well, because even though I'm fifteen, I already know I'm going to be a famous writer one day like Mark Twain, George Bernard Shaw, or Anaïs Nin. They kept diaries, too. So did Dostoyevsky when he wasn't standing on high window ledges and chugalugging vodka. Besides, I did a lot of thinking tonight, and I know this coming summer is going to be one of staggering importance. This might end up being a record of my aching final pubescence. Several other events have also occurred recently which made me start this.

A) I had my first wet dream a week ago Wednesday. As a child, I also walked and talked late.

B) Two months ago my mother, Mrs. Brenda Dingman, rented our cellar to a man called Charlie Mayo who walks with a limp and wheezes like a godfather. Right after that my mother started wearing a lot of makeup for the first time since almost six years ago when my father moved out of our lower-middle-class split-level and went to live with a statuesque secretary in NoHo, which is south of Ray's Pizza in Manhattan's Greenwich Village.

C) I got another "A" from my benevolent English teacher, Miss Elena Racinski, for a short story I wrote on the sophomore final called "The Perfect Sleeping Room."

D) My sister, Penelope, came home from New Paltz State Teachers' College to look for a job to work herself through her last three years because my father stopped sending her money like he had promised. My mother took him to court, but he's a policeman so he contributes only $11.53 a month to Penelope and me each as child support because he knew the judge. He also got to keep the Toyota hatchback in the divorce settlement, which he traded in for a maroon Chrysler New Yorker with power windows.

E) The *Bayonne News & Sun,* to which I subscribe, carried a front-page story that gave me nightmares. The

2

Tuesday headline announced, MARILYN MONROE'S GHOST TALKS TO PRESIDENTIAL AIDE.

F) And, I suppose, the very most recent event which made me start this diary is that tonight, after my spoon-throwing Oedipal outbreak, my mom called my aunt Ruth, who's very big in the cushy New York State Employment Agency hierarchy, and got me a summer job as a waiter at The Lake Henry Hotel, which is two hundred and twenty-six miles north of here, in the primitive Adirondack Mountains.

Thursday, June 27

Helen Keller was born on this day in 1880.

Things are coming down on me fast and heavy now, and I don't know if I can get my thoughts down as fast as I should. I mean, I don't have it as bad as Helen Keller, but I finally apologized to my mom before lunch and she told me not to worry about it, that Charlie-in-the-cellar had told her the facts about what it's like to be a boy whose father long ago walked out on him. She said she really understood me better now and that I'd really love the Adirondacks. She told me Aunt Ruth had called with a list of the things I'd need for my position at the hotel and that I'd be taking a Greyhound Bus at 9:22 A.M. tomorrow. The hotel's only open summers, she stressed, and I'd be back right after Labor Day. After breakfast, we walked down to the Bayonne Mall, and she bought me a pair of black cotton pants and joined the Swift Diet Club. She said she was tired of being sixty pounds overweight, and bought seven boxes of Wasa Lite Rye crackers, a pound bag of imitation bacon-flavored crunchies and a bottle each of vitamins C, E and B-stress tablets. There was something about the pace of the whole thing that made me feel she was glad to get rid of me. I made some reference to child labor laws, but she told me Aunt Ruth said everything was legal and millions of other high school students would give their right ears to trade places with me for the hotel administration experience I was going to get. We also went to Waldenbooks where she bought herself a paperback copy of Gail Sheehy's *Passages* and a low-cal Italian cookbook. I bought *The Last of the Mohicans* and a dozen other classics.

I stayed the whole afternoon in my room. Today's *Bayonne News & Sun* had shocking preview photos of Sylvester Stallone in his birthday suit. The headline said, RAMBO IN THE BUFFO NOT SO BOFFO! It's shocking how many Hollywood and rock stars are turning up without any clothes on these days. Either that or they're getting apprehended at Heathrow for trying to smuggle drugs stashed in VHS cassette cartridges. Frankly, I was very depressed, and at one point I felt moisture in my eyes even though I don't cry. Most of the time I just sat on my bed surrounded by my books and records, taking a good look at myself in the mirror. I'm really a good-looking kid, with blond hair and no pimples, and I have a Water Pik. If I were a father or mother, I'd really like to keep me around.

I played half the score to *South Pacific,* three songs by Madonna and all of *Night on Bald Mountain.* Then I called Calvin Kennedy and told him I was leaving tomorrow for the whole summer. He told me he'd really like to come over and say good-bye, but he was throwing up in bed with a 104° fever. An hour later I looked out the window and saw him speed by in a convertible with Jake Cahill and his older brother, Flick. Calvin was screaming "Great melons!" to a girl walking down the street, and he didn't look very sick.

During dinner I got very depressed watching Charlie-from-the-cellar devour a huge plate of dietetic vermicelli. Everything about the dinner was a downer. My mother drank five 8-ounce glasses of water and kept trying to look demure as she sampled everyone's meatballs. My sister, Penelope, looked exhausted from a day of job hunting. She said she had filled out applications for Ma Bell, Allied Chemical Corporation, a Newark day-care center, and the Bayonne 5 & 10-cent dry goods store, where everything costs a minimum of two dollars. I know Penelope didn't mean it, but she said she never wanted to see our father again and she wouldn't care if he got his head shot off in a fast-food-store payroll heist. She said if all cops were like him, she'd emigrate down under, where they "put another shrimp on the barbie, mate!" After all these years, I'm the only one who still misses him.

Friday, June 28

1) World War I ended with the signing of the Treaty of Versailles on this day in 1919.

2) Great headlines in the newspaper:

A) KISSING LOWERS YOUR CHOLESTEROL

B) MYTHS YOUR MARRIAGE CAN DO WITHOUT

C) POPE SPEAKS OUT ON ROCK AND ROLL VISION OF YOKO ONO

Mom made sure I was packed on the train to New York early. Then I made the 9:22 Adirondack bus from the Port Authority terminal in plenty of time. The schedule includes stops mainly at Tarrytown, Nyack, Bear Mountain, Albany, Lake Henry, and Lake Champlain. Mom made me a breakfast of waffles, bacon, and a chocolate shake in the blender. She acted like she couldn't cook me enough food. She packed me a snack pack of one apple, two tangelos, a granola bar, one Chunky, a raspberry-jam sandwich and three Snickers candy bars. She also gave me $27 for the bus ticket, but she thought I should use my own savings of $16.42 from a brief aluminum-can-redemption career as money to hold me over till I get my first paycheck or tips from hotel customers. Penelope slipped me a twenty-dollar bill of her own. She couldn't have had much left after that. I tried to make her take it back, but she said it was nothing and she'd write to me. The most unpleasant thing that happened was Charlie popping his head out of the cellar and calling ''Ciao'' as I went down the street, lugging my brown Samsonite. It looks like the kind of luggage the gorilla throws around in a cage on that TV commercial. I think my mother showed some signs of regret in the final moments of our farewell when she told me she'd miss me at dinner. She said she was only having a chef salad without the ham and cheese for herself, but she was going to make baked ziti for everyone else. Mom actually looked pretty in the early-morning light. She has her hair cut like Peter Pan, but streaked, and a sensitive, mature face like Olivia Newton-John.

I knew right away the Greyhound Bus driver was a

crank. He had a snotty look and was rude to everyone before the bus even got out of New York. He spoke on the P.A. system, giving minimal information: "YOU WILL HAVE EXACTLY THIRTY-TWO MINUTES AT THE RED APPLE REST. THOSE NOT BACK IN THE BUS WILL BE LEFT BEHIND." As the bus moved down the ramp and began to leave the city, I kept getting flashes of Mom and Penelope. An Oriental lady was sitting on the aisle seat next to me staring at my teeth. She was eating something that looked like tofu, with either bean sprouts or white worms. My stomach felt funny as it was, and even when the highway started to get attractive up past Grant's Tomb and the George Washington Bridge, I knew I was extra severely depressed. I felt like I was dying. I felt like banging my head against the window. For a while, I had an urge to indulge in scream therapy. I felt the same way when I was nine and my father packed up and moved out. I didn't want to leave Bayonne. I hated leaving Mom. I hated leaving Penelope. I knew we had secrets to share if we'd only had enough time to get down to it. Someone had a boom box on the bus and was playing a cassette of Julio Iglesias. I began to thank God I had already sent an address change for my subscription to the *Bayonne News & Sun*. I brought a total of seventeen books with me. My suitcase almost ripped my right arm off, but I had vowed the summer wouldn't retard my intellectual growth.

Specifically, I brought my *Mentor Pocket Dictionary, History of the World, The Compleat Book of Famous Births and Deaths,* a thick paperback called *Genius Through the Ages,* Marcel Proust's *Swann's Way,* Samuel Knight's *The Return of the Hero,* Masters and John son's *Sexual Inadequacy, The Rise and Fall of Philosophy,*

Ship of Fools, Hamlet, seven other classics, *Peterson's Quotes and Proverbs,* and two *Mad* magazines.

It's funny, but now, after just a little while of writing in this diary, I feel better. Not much. Actually, I just realized if I keep writing every day and recording all the things that assault me this summer, I'll probably turn out an important record of my times. Someday afrer I die this journal might be the object of a crazed bidding war between international dealers. Besides, there are so many things I want to write down just for posterity.

"The charm of the journal must consist in a certain greenness and not in maturity. Here I cannot afford to be remembering what I said or did, but what I am and aspire to become."—Henry David Thoreau

Saturday, June 29

I'm in my room at the employees' dormitory and on the verge of nervous disintegration. I've got to fight to stay awake long enough to at least shorthand the horrors that have bombarded me since I got off the bus last night.

The mean driver let me out in Loudon's Landing, which turned out to be on the west stretch of Lake Henry and the hick town closest to the hotel. From what I could see, Loudon's Landing consists of a post office, an underprivileged mall, one bakery, and eighteen bars. The saloon right in front of me was called Hairy Mary's Place, and it had a yellow Budweiser beer sign of a tiny illusionary waterfall flickering in the window. I could see several mountaineers perched at the bar. Then an old man who looked like a flannel-plaid bear walked by, and I asked directions to The Lake Henry Hotel. He pointed me down a dark road called Skunks Misery Lane. I thanked him.

As I walked along, I noticed two raccoons sitting on a plastic garbage can across the street and at least three other pairs of beady eyes staring at me from bushes and huge pine trees, which were all over the place. It was cool and smelled very fresh. Only the better senior citizens' parks in Bayonne have that much foliage. Then, after a few hundred yards, the moon jumped out and lit up a huge lake and a very small bridge. I also saw a sign announcing "The Lake Henry Hotel." The bridge wasn't more than fifteen feet above the water and only as long as the distance between two telephone poles. The whole thing looked like the start of a third remake of *The Night of the Living Dead*. A wind came up and a night mist crept in from the lake. I watched my shadow follow me, and I held tight to my suitcase as ahead of me was a small, black island. I can't write anymore now because everything after that got awful.

Sunday, June 30, 11:15 P.M.

Can't write. I think I'm growing a major zit on my left nostril. I am in a state of shock.

Monday, July 1, Midnight

Still can't write.

Tuesday, July 2

1) Ernest Hemingway committed suicide on this day in 1961, according to my book on famous births and deaths.

2) I can't let everything get me down. I'm determined to bring my journal up-to-date. I think some people at the hotel are potential killers, so this may become an important document in a court case investigating my murder. If anyone finds this, Penelope will know what to do with it.

Highlights of the rest of the night I arrived were:

A) Skunks Misery Lane led onto the island but then quickly forked where a big sign pointed "GUESTS" in one direction and "EMPLOYEES" in the other.

B) I ended up at the employees' dormitory, which was a humongous converted turkey barn. It was three stories high, and I didn't have to be Juan Valdez the coffee sniffer to tell there was a vile cesspool nearby.

C) Mrs. Brady, a lady shaped like a gourd and wearing a fright wig, was sitting on the front porch guarding the dormitory lobby. She announced she was the custodial person and checked me in. She told me the right side was for all the male employees and the left side was for all the female employees and never the twain shall meet.

D) She gave me two sheets with holes in them, one sample bar of Ivory Soap and a key to Room 208. She said I was lucky, because I almost ended up having to share a room with a dipsomaniacal bellhop, but when she read on the day's new employees' arrival sheet that I was only fifteen, she gave me the last single. I said I didn't know how to thank her, and she said she liked Fanny Farmer chocolate-peanut turtles and Genoa salami.

E) As Mrs. Brady was getting me squared away, I noticed a huge collection of mankind and womankind lounging on mutilated Naugahyde sofas and ripped, overstuffed chairs. Some of these off-duty employees looked really exhausted and were still wearing waitress and waiter uniforms. Others were in jeans and loud, motley shirts with flamingos on them. They looked every age from seventeen to seventy, smoking, drinking, and watching a rerun of Alexis and Krystle Carrington hair pulling in a fish pond. The only *Homo sapiens* I'd ever seen who looked like these employees were perfume salesgirls, used-car salesmen, and unemployed ballroom-dance instructors.

"You eat breakfast at the zoo at 7 A.M. sharp," Mrs. Brady told me. "Then report to the maître d', Alfredo."

"What's the zoo?"

"The employees' cafeteria," she said, as though I was the most retarded person she'd ever met.

F) My room was a slum the size of a closet. It had mildewed roses and cracked midget angels as the wallpaper design.

11

G) I could hear guys playing cards and slurping beverages in the rooms down the hall.

H) My mattress was hard as ice. As I made my bed and unpacked my suitcase, I had the distinct feeling I didn't have to worry about anyone stealing my literature. There was a naked 60-watt light bulb which swung from the ceiling. I wanted to disappear. I was cold. My body was shaking. I wanted to be back home in Bayonne. I wanted to be with my mother. I wanted Penelope. Even my best friend, Calvin Kennedy, the liar. I wanted anything. If this was what the world was going to be like, I wanted to metamorphose into a giant cockroach like the guy in Kafka's famous story. I decided to start reading *Madame Bovary* by Gustave Flaubert.

Wednesday, July 3

God bless the *Bayonne Sun & News*. I received three back copies in the mail today. Reading about the provocative tribulations of other people has given me strength. The main stories were:

1) MAD MOTHER FLUSHES THREE THOUSAND DOLLARS OF HER SON'S MONEY DOWN TOILET WHEN SHE MARRIES A HARE KRISHNA

2) EVIL GROOM TORTURES BRIDE WITH POISON TOADS

3) ALIEN CREW LIVES AFTER UFO CRASH IN BOISE, IDAHO

I'm so excited about news from the outside reaching me, I can go on with my diary. Maybe I can really bring it up-to-date.

When my first morning at the dormitory came I didn't need my calculator watch to wake me up. The noise from the hall sounded like a gaggle of gibbons in Dolby sound. I got out of bed, put on my black shoes, black socks, black pants, white shirt and black bow tie and staggered to a hall bathroom. I managed to fight my way to a sink and brush my teeth. Then I struggled down the creaking stairs and through the dorm lobby toward the bright sunlight that hit the porch. I didn't have to wonder where the zoo was, because there was a paved path filled with a rushing horde of employees dressed in uniforms. It looked like a march of mutant Amazon ants, and I got swept along with them. I began to breathe the cool morning air, and for the first time, I could see how really giant Lake Henry and the hotel were. It was one of the most beautiful sights I'd ever seen. The hotel's island wasn't more than a quarter of a mile long, but the guest rooms and dining room were in a gigantic structure of white wood. It was very Victorian, with lots of different levels of roofs and shutters. From certain angles, it looked 'ike an albino octopus with a rotunda at the center and four arms that stretched out to grip the southern tip of the island. The whole place had to be over a hundred years old. The front of the octopus even had a huge colonnade that looked like Mount Vernon warped into a semicircle. A gigantic lawn rolled down to a swimming pool and a huge, white guest dock. It was obviously the kind of place rich, suave persons stay at.

The beauty ended when I followed everyone through a screen door underneath the rear left corner of the hotel. This was the zoo. I got on line, picked up a tray, tin utensils and a cheap, stiff, paper napkin that felt just like the ones they give at the Bayonne High cafeteria.

This place was worse. A hundred workers at a clip had to eat there, and the area is only the size of a portable classroom.

The choice of food that morning was:

a) a bowl of hot mush

b) fried eggs that looked like Cyclops eyes

c) cold toast with congealed orange marmalade

d) all the powdered milk you could drink

e) decaying coffee

f) pork sausages in the shape of fried fingers

g) an individual box of Froot Loops

The people serving behind the steam tables and replenishing the salt, pepper, and Sanka packets looked like they were recruited from the Barbary Coast. In fact, I don't want to write anything more about the zoo just now or my diary will be endangered by uncontrollable reverse peristalsis. I drank a glass of milk and decided I'd better report for duty. I hardly had to move my feet. The ant army was in constant flow now through an ugly passageway. The odors struck me as a mixture of Johnson's baby powder, dead eels, and Old Spice. We had to file right by a heavy-duty machine that was shining silverware by bouncing it over ball bearings.

Then we all clomped up a staircase and at the top went through a doorway that let us loose into the biggest kitchen in the universe. This place looked like it could have made all the Hungarian goulash for World War II. The other waiters, waitresses, bellhops, maids, and everybody else broke away from the pack here and started dashing in all sorts of directions. Some were manning specific culinary battle stations. There was so much motion I felt a severe anxiety attack coming on. I know a lot of geniuses get them, so I didn't mind too much. I read Freud used to faint like clockwork. I was so dazed I thought I was having an out-of-body experience. Then I realized I was only seeing my reflections in several 50-gallon stainless steel mixing bowls hanging with dozens of other huge vats over my head. I looked pathetic. My hair hung straight down over my ears like drenched watercress. At that moment, I just felt so ugly and fatigued I needed a sugar fix. I asked myself, who did I think I was kidding? I was a dodo. An inadequate person. I was manically depressed. I was suffocating under an indoor sky of pots. I couldn't stand myself. You're a bore, I said to me. You're puny. You're lacking in quality, like a pair of factory-rejected Fruit of the Loom shorts. And this was without considering any sexual problems, since I've never had sex with anyone except myself.

I can't write anymore now. It's very late. I have to go to sleep. Good night, Dear Diary. Maybe I'll get a letter from Mom or Penelope soon, but not tomorrow because it's a legal holiday.

Thursday, July 4, 3:30 A.M.—
Independence Day

I can't sleep, so I'll write a little bit more. I still want to get the ugly part over with. Also some of the really critical occurrences.

That first morning when I arrived in the main hotel kitchen somebody spoke to me.

"You're a new waiter, aren't you?" the squeaky voice inquired, penetrating my spastic condition. I turned to see a short, old Indian waving his right hand in little

15

circles and smiling at me. He wasn't an American Indian. He was one of those Bombay ones who come from the place where thousands of people still die of cobra bites.

"Yes," I said, noticing he had several other Indians working with him at a long machine that appeared to be an aquatic crematorium. One of them flicked a switch, and the machine started to *swuuuusssh* and blast water and steam in all directions. The other Indians shoved racks of dirty glasses in one end, and they'd come out the other end clean. It was really a twenty-foot-long car wash for dirty dishes.

"I'm Mahatma," the old Indian introduced himself, and then he pointed to two of the other Indians and told me their names were something like Buddhakariskaman and Buddhafatima. I knew right off I'd remember Mahatma, but the other two didn't stand a chance. Besides, the way he carried himself I could tell he was the boss of the washing machine crew. The others just smiled and did bowing motions and kept shoving racks of glasses and dishes into the gurgling machine.

Mahatma deduced I needed help. First thing he did was whirl his hand in a little circle again and tell me to wait. It was a really weird gesture. But he got me a pea-green waiter's jacket from a linen closet. I had seen the other waiters carrying them and putting them on, so I figured I'd be ending up with one eventually. Mahatma also gave me a cummerbund and said I'd have to wear it, too. I'd seen those on men at weddings. They're shiny, wide, beltlike things that help hide potbellies.

"That's Alfredo," Mahatma said, pointing to a smooth-looking Latino guy around thirty-five in a tux. "You have to see him."

Alfredo was standing outside a little glass booth talk-

16

ing to a tall man dressed in a white starched jacket and a two-foot-high puffed-out chef's hat.

I thanked Mahatma and made a beeline to Alfredo. At a discreet moment I interrupted and told him that my aunt Ruth from the New York State Employment Agency had sent me. There was something nice about him, because I could see he wanted to laugh right in my face, but he only smiled and told me I'd be "following Scotty" for a couple of days and then I'd be on my own. Alfredo had a Spanish accent, which turned out to be Cuban, but he was very sophisticated and walked like a jaguar wearing pomade. Alfredo introduced me to Head Chef O'Hara, the guy he was talking to, who up close had a bulbous nose and looked like W. C. Fields with a doozy of a hangover. Then Alfredo snapped his fingers and this young waiter, Scotty, zipped over. Scotty was normal looking, about twenty years old, pleasant, and seemed a touch brain damaged. It was either that or he just didn't talk very fast, but I had a hard time listening so slowly as he took me on a tour of the kitchen.

THE HIGHLIGHTS OF MY KITCHEN TOUR WERE:

1) Waiters and waitresses running around with big aluminum trays carrying food out through a set of swinging doors.

2) The salad section.

3) The griddle section.

4) The bakery section.

5) The broiler section.

The woman or guy in charge of each section was each a character who boggled the mind, but I think I'll wait until I know them better before putting my impressions of them straight into this diary. The only guy I knew right away I'd hate was the assistant broiler chef, who was a young punk called Bunker. When Scotty introduced me, Bunker howled and puckered up his lips, making loud vulgar sounds at me. "Oh, you're cute, Snooks," he said as he was throwing kippers on the flames. Smoke was rising all around him. Just the way he looked at me made my stomach turn. He wore a sweat-catching bandana, and more perspiration dripped down his T-shirt and tight-fitting button-fly Levi's. He couldn't have been more than eighteen, and what was worse, he had the sharp, swarthy looks of a pizza thrower and body language that broadcasted he thought he was God's gift to girls. The head grill man didn't tell him to stop making fun of me because he himself looked like a raving Mongolian. The rest of the whole griddle and grill runway looked like sumo wrestlers, including one woman who was in charge of making pancakes. They just snickered while Bunker kept making vulgar sounds and calling me "Snooks." Scotty told me to forget about it and led me around a corner to introduce me to the mysteries of a boiling cauldron with chains and tin cups. It was the soft-boiled-egg timer, but I was too trembly to concentrate.

4 A.M.—Still the Beginning of Independence Day

I'm almost caught up, because the rest of what happened the first few days has been shoved into my unconscious. There's just a few more facts I need to jot down before I can go to sleep and then get up and go to the zoo for my next gag-me-to-the-max breakfast.

A) The Lake Henry dining room is at least 500 feet long and serves 1,500 guests per sitting. It has picture windows all looking out on its incredible lawn and splendiferous lake that look like Paradise.

B) I learned how to set a table with salt, pepper, sugar, ashtrays, forks, knives, spoons, glasses, bread plates, relish dishes, cloth napkins, and flowers. At home my mom believed in simpler settings.

C) Today the hotel officially stops hosting conventions for groups like the Daughters of the American Revolution and Metropolitan Life Insurance. The fancy big social season begins. No more cut-rate prices for capitalistic businesses or freaky organizations.

D) In three and a half hours I will be a waiter on my own. God help my guests.

10:06 P.M.—The Last Hours of the 4th of July

My first day as a waiter is over. My life will never be the same. I have seen Heaven and I have seen Hell.

First, the Hell part.

By lunchtime, Alfredo, the maître d', had appointed me to my "station" in the massive dining room. If I were a terrific, experienced waiter, he'd have given me one of the best stations, along the picture windows, where I'd get the richest customers and biggest tips. Scotty told me it also helps a lot if a waiter gives Alfredo kickbacks on tips. Sort of a caloric tithing. I got the worst station. It consists of one big, round table that seats ten and another table that seats four, with a main view of a rooftop air conditioner. The worst stations are always the farthest from the kitchen, too, which means I'll always have to run the length of a football field to serve a tomato juice. My round table is called a "stag" table because swinging socialite singles are assigned there so they can meet each other and strike up chic relationships during their stay. I know my income won't be bad because each guest gets a card when they check in that says *MINIMUM TIPPING: twenty-five cents each for breakfast and lunch, and fifty cents for dinner.* That means a dollar a day per customer, and if I have fourteen I'll end up making fourteen dollars a day, which is a lot more than I've ever earned for doing anything in Bayonne. They're supposed to give me the loot when they check out. Other facts and guidelines from Scotty are:

1) Guests can order as much of anything on the menu they want. If a person feels like it they can make me serve them a breakfast of twenty-three half grapefruits, eighteen eggs, twenty-nine rashers of bacon, four omelettes, a gallon of coffee and seventy cheese Danish with a dozen blintzes.

2) Every lunch will be a huge buffet set out on a long table with an ice sculpture of a sailfish or mermaid where guests take an empty plate and make selections from hundreds of platters and bowls that contain things like cold lobster tails, duck, goose pâtés, vegetable salads, meat salads, ambrosia, bagels, rolls, fresh cut beef, ham, midget corns, endless cheeses, creamed herring, frogs' legs, fried chicken, dill pickles, stuffed artichokes, Nova Scotia salmon, marinated mushrooms, papayas, garbanzo beans, hot, exotic casseroles, Mandarin oranges, wild rice with pistachios, cold pasta with

spinach, mangoes and pomegranates, plus a lot of other junk I can't remember.

3) At lunch all I have to do is serve the beverage, which can be a choice of iced tea, coffee, or something else simple. Special waiters handle the booze orders, so the guests pay separate for that.

4) Dinner is again as much as a guest can eat, and every Saturday night is steak night. Sunday's always check-out and check-in day for anyone leaving or arriving.

5) I forgot to record that guests can also devour as many desserts as they want. The desserts are usually strawberry shortcake, chocolate mousse, seventeen flavors of ice cream, New York cheesecake with raspberry brandy topping, petit fours, oozing eclairs, bananas flambé, Napoleons, whipped egg whites with brandy, vanilla custard, Boston cream pie, lady fingers, chocolate-dipped fruits, foot-high butter-cream cakes, candy truffles, English trifles, mints, and forty or fifty other things.

6) Waiters are forbidden to eat any food except from the zoo.

After breakfast almost all the final convention of the Daughters of the American Revolution checked out. That meant the big oval at the hotel's main entrance pretty much emptied of Fords and Mazdas, and as lunchtime approached they were replaced by BMWs, Mercedeses, and Rolls Royces, because the richer "social season guests" started arriving. The first guest Alfredo seated at my stag table was a distinguished forty-year-old lady who looked like Dr. Joyce Brothers but wasn't. Then he seated a couple of younger women who acted very snooty, but I think they were really secretaries who had saved up and were planning to entrap rich male Yuppies. Alfredo also gave me one of the last Daughters of the American Revolution, who would only be staying for lunch. There was space because a lot of the rich people were still driving in from Nantucket and places like Lockjaw Ridge, I was told. This last "Daughter" was very nice and called me by my name since I was wearing a compulsory plastic nameplate on my green leprechaun's jacket. I had printed "Eugene" in very big letters so no one would have any trouble making out their tip envelopes on Sundays. Out of my fourteen seats I ended up with only four customers for lunch, but something very revolting happened.

It officially started when the Daughter of the American Revolution wanted a special fruit cup from the kitchen—one with kiwi fruit and coconut shreds, which was a featured item the night before, but she so loved it she begged me to see if there was any left. I told her there wasn't, because I didn't feel like walking the length of a football field, but my immediate supervisor, Captain Pegeen O'Halloran, told me to go to the kitchen and ask. The chain of command in the dining room was shaping up to be Alfredo the maître d' at the top, and then a weird-looking Adirondack assistant maître d' called Louie who helps Alfredo milk tips out of people for the better tables. But there are also eleven captains below them, who each are in charge of about ten waiters or so. Anyway, mine is Captain Pegeen O'Halloran, who is in her forties and looks very demure and Irish, with eight bizarre braids. Scotty warned me he knew her from other seasons and that she was famous for sucking side tips out of guests by making her waiters look one quart low. No one had to tell me she was the most inept captain, because she has the worst section of waiters—which means she has mine. Anyway, thanks to Captain Pegeen I had to take my big aluminum tray and march into the kitchen and ask the salad chef if he had a kiwi fruit salad left over for the lady. The salad chef said *yes*, and while I was waiting for him to fix it, Bunker came over from the broiler section. At first it looked like he wanted to be friends. He wasn't even sweaty and looked borderline normal. He smiled. I really wanted him to like me, because he wasn't much older than I and without the vapors he even looked more like a pleasant Cro-Magnon Matt Dillon than a swarthy pizza thrower.

"Hi, Bunker," I said.

"Hi, *Snooks*," he said.

"I wish you'd just call me Eugene," I told him nicely.

"Okay, Snooks," he replied.

Bunker watched the salad chef shove a Kiwi Delight at me, and I had to supreme it, which means put it in an individual ice bowl. It is really very semi-French service I'm expected to perform. I had to scoop my own crushed ice, put a silver holder on top of the bowl, set the bowl on a small plate with a doily and then put the salad cup on top of that. With prune juice and tomato juice I have to put a lemon wedge on the side as well. Actually, everything about being a waiter at The Lake Henry Hotel is designed to bust chops.

"What is that, Snooks?" Bunker asked.

"A kiwi salad," I answered, still trying to be civilized. "It's for one of the Daughters of the American Revolution that didn't check out yet."

"Gee, I'm impressed."

"You are?"

"Yeah, Snooks."

And then he leaned over and *spit* in the salad.

I gagged. Not that it was a giant, colossal glob or anything like that. It was just sort of more like a spray from his lips that hit the top slices of kiwi like a shot of Windex.

"Why did you do that?" I inquired.

"Because I felt like it."

"You're disgusting."

"You think so, Snooks?"

"Yes, I think so."

"Well, then *you* eat it!"

Before I could stop him, Bunker grabbed my neck and started pushing my head down toward the polluted kiwis. I gave him an elbow in his ribs, but he was too strong for me. He laughed while I squirmed with his hand clamped on the back of my head. Right now all I can remember about that moment is that something magical happened. As I was twisting to get loose I was aware of the salad chef ignoring the whole matter and laying out hundreds of half pears on Boston lettuce leaves as pre-preparation for the evening meal. That wasn't the magical part. I also caught sight of old, brown-skinned Mahatma far across the kitchen next to the car wash for dishes, his Indian eyes dead set at me like lasers. That still wasn't the enchanting part. That part was that the most beautiful ghost I've ever seen in my life floated by. From the position of my vibrating head I knew the spirit was a young female with a face more beautiful than Yolande Betbeze, who was a Miss America and visited near Bayonne once. There was all whiteness, an aura of electricity and a faint scent of lavender. I felt my knees go out from under me. I really think my telescoping toward the floor had nothing to do with Bunker ramming me down with his arm. The ghost spoke scoldingly as it passed. It said, "Let him go, Bunker." The voice was so celestial it made my eardrums twang like harp strings. I didn't care if Bunker killed me at that moment because I was seeing and hearing Heaven.

In a split second the ghost had floated out of the kitchen and through the swinging doors to the dining room. She was gone. Bunker let me go. As I staggered to my feet Captain Pegeen swooped into view and grabbed the kiwi salad off my tray.

"What is taking so long?" she wanted to know. In a flash she ran off with the salad. I hurried after her, warning, "Don't! Bunker spit in it!"

All Bunker did was whistle as I chased after Captain Pegeen through the doors into the dining room.

Still bedazzled, I took half the football field to catch up with her. My mind and eyes spun crazily on a dozen different schizoid levels. I knew the "ghost" had to be a waitress I'd never seen before. I desperately wanted to see the vision again, and yet I knew I had a higher moral purpose at the moment.

"Bunker spit in the salad," I repeated to Captain Pegeen, this time a desperate whisper smack into her moving ear.

"It looks just fine," she said.

Before I could stop her, she flashed a phony smile and gracefully flew the kiwi salad in front of the septua-genarian Daughter of the American Revolution.

"Isn't that nice of you!" the lady exclaimed to Captain Pegeen, like I didn't even exist.

"My pleasure." Captain Pegeen beamed.

"But . . ." I muttered.

Captain Pegeen spun to face me with her petrifying eyes and dyed-amber braids fanned out like a Gaelic Medusa. She grabbed my arm and marched me away while the woman began to munch on the kiwis.

"What's your problem?" Captain Pegeen grilled.

"I told you Bunker spit in that salad!"

"Look, nothing's perfect," she growled. "And you'd better get that through your head if you're going to make it around here!"

I was stunned. She left me standing by my tray stand and zipped back to the stags with her expansive phony smile plastered back on her face.

"Tasty?" she inquired of the Daughter of the American Revolution.

"Oh my, *yes!*" the lady sighed, licking her lips.

And now, Dear Diary, I must write specifically about the Heaven part. What happened then was that I looked across the aisle from my station and saw the beautiful poltergeist who had ordered Bunker to let me go. My hand is shaking even now as I write what I saw:

The ghost was a waitress in a shimmering white, Dacron polyester, wash 'n' wear uniform. The sun streamed down on her from the picture window behind her. Her hair was long, raven in color, and she had gorgeous dark slashes for eyebrows. Her skin was white and her eyes were as lovely and vulnerable as a baby cheetah's. What was most remarkable was she also looked like she had a high I.Q. It was an hour ago, and already my thoughts are leaping about in my brain like neon tetras in a fish tank. She was really more striking than any beauty queen. She looked about sixteen or seventeen. Her alertness was like Madame Curie's. I couldn't focus on one part of her at a time. Her entire being radiated across the forty feet between us. She was a sparkling sorceress, busy tending the guests at her prime station. She served skim milk like Cleopatra. She removed a dish like Helen of Troy. I was mesmerized. I was intoxicated.

I *am* in love! I love her more than a *Vogue* model. More than Meryl Streep. Or Cher. Or Molly Ringwald. And I've only found out two things about her.

1) Her name is Della.

2) She's Bunker's girlfriend.

I'm exhausted. I need sleep.

Friday, July 5, 5:03 A.M.

A) Today makes exactly six years since my father moved out to go live with the statuesque secretary.

B) National holiday in Venezuela.

C) I've now read 83 pages of *Madame Bovary* by Gustave Flaubert.

I'm awake. I did nothing but dream about Della. Now I must set down the real Hell and shame that fell on me at last night's dinner before I block it out completely. It made the spit in the kiwis seem like a kiss of dew. From the moment I saw Della I used every excuse to follow her. If she went to the kitchen, I went to the kitchen. After lunch when she went to get water glasses, I went to get water glasses. I kept a fair distance from her, did my best to make certain no one would notice me following her. Only Mahatma saw me when I was in a second hypnotic trance near the egg timer and Della was using an ice scoop near the pantry freezer. I pretended I didn't see him watching me, but when I brought my dirty silverware out for washing he made his usual weird circle motion in the air with his right hand and chuckled.

"She's very beautiful," he whispered.

"Who?" I asked.

Mahatma smiled and started helping me stack my knives and forks and stuff in a rack. I didn't look him in the eye. Actually, I looked at his shirt, which was a freaky complicated design. In the main chest area it had an embroidered yellow urn, and around it were water-colored crocodiles and a lot of mysterious mutant sea creatures. I noticed all of the Indians working with him had very foreign-looking clothing as bright as rainbows, with designs like squirrels eating nuts with other squirrels coveting them. One of them was wearing a robelike get-up that had a picture of an emperor dying of opium addiction. No standard white uniforms for Mahatma's little group, that much I have to say.

It was Scotty who eventually told me Della's name and that she was going out with Bunker.

Now after lunch the dining-room staff usually can manage a three- or four-hour break, depending on how long it takes to set up for dinner. Since it was my first evening setup on my own it took me extra long. The experienced waiters and waitresses know how to beat everybody out and grab clean tablecloths and silverware so they don't have to wait on line. It took me forever. I barely got back to my room when I had to turn around and go to the zoo for my own chow, which was a meat loaf that tasted like ground beef brains and marinated kangaroo heart. I was nervous. I couldn't wait to see Della again. I wanted to do spectacularly well that night because she would see me. But it wasn't just I who was tense. The entire hotel staff was excited and hyped up, like it was Academy Awards night or the Super Bowl. The front oval now was completely swamped with only ritzy cars. Word spread fast it was a full house. Guests were strolling all over the grounds. They had on expensive gowns and dinner jackets and even fur-trimmed things. The hotel's eight-piece orchestra was playing "I Could Have Danced All Night" and a cha-cha version of a Chopin étude. Even merengues and sambas. Long before the dining-room doors opened for the first eaters it was as if the whole Lake Henry Hotel was starting to make one loud sound. It built up stronger and stronger, actually reverberating in the wooden floors of the kitchen. Finally it became a deafening pounding, and by then it was the sound of my heart. Everyone zipped around faster and faster. Waiters were hoarding underliners and doilies for fruit juices at the tray stands. Waitresses were putting on hairnets and butterfly clips. The head chef was swigging gin in his glass booth. He had on a fresh white uniform and higher puffed hat. The subchefs were setting up foodstuffs. Assistants were grating cheese, making gravies, tossing lettuces. The grill midway looked like Purgatory itself, with the crew stoking fires and precooking meats and sauces. They arranged pitchers of ice water and had opened their shirts to look like hairy apes. Bunker was so wide-eyed and crazed preparing fillet of soles he didn't even notice me. His entire mental faculties were fish and flame directed. I couldn't imagine Della with such a primate. Oh God, then I heard the flood of guests burst into the dining room. I ran out to see a stream of diamond necklaces, stiff coiffures, sequinned dresses, and penguin tuxedos jockeying for table assignments from Maître d' Alfredo and his flunky Assistant Maître d' Louie.

I reached my tables and trembled. Suddenly, Della materialized at her station. She looked cool, relaxed. She had her hair pulled into a dignified ponytail like Diana the Moon Goddess. I had another fantasy that at the end of the evening she'd cross over from her station and say, "Hello, Eugene. I'm very impressed by your expertise as a waiter."

That wasn't in the stars.

The Dr. Brothers look-alike arrived at my stag table first. She was wearing a gold dress with no shoulders. My other two official women guests from lunch showed up wearing very thin mink stoles. Moments later, Louie seated four new women, who looked more authentically well-heeled, and I decided they were all divorcées. They had a few cocktails under their beaded blouses and were really in full throttle. One looked like Jill Clayburgh, but wasn't. The others looked like Princess Di, Jacqueline Bisset, and Tina Turner. The routine was that I had to give them each a little menu and an order card, and they had to write out everything they wanted. In seconds, they were busy scribbling away and saying, "Good evening, Eugene," and laughing and whirling their heads to look at any stag male guests coming down the aisle. I could feel considerable tension building at the table between the different factions of women. I peeked over their shoulders and began to get rattled when I saw they were all having different things to begin with. One wrote *capers and endive*. Another wrote *prune juice*. Another, the *anchovy* appetizer. The other orders were a *tomato juice*, a *shrimp cocktail*, one *papaya* and one *cranapple juice*. I grabbed my tray and ran to the kitchen, snatched up the seven appetizers, supremed what had to be supremed, remembered the lemons for the prune and tomato juices and got back to the table before the seven had even finished writing down everything they wanted. I was way ahead of the game as I collected the cards and *whooooshed* the appetizers in front of them.

"What wonderful service, Eugene," Princess Di said.

"Thank you."

But then the assistant maître d', Louie, who, I forgot to mention, now looked like a backwoods answer to James Cagney in a powder-blue zoot-suit jacket, seated two more ladies at my table. They looked like Twiggy and Bella Abzug types. Twiggy was younger and prettier than the others, so she got a lot of dirty stares, and the whole pack of nine stag ladies knew there was only one seat left for a man. I mean, they didn't let their anxiety show every second. It was more of a giggling frenzy that broke out, especially when Assistant Maître d' Louie finally seated a man with them who looked like Harrison Ford. You could really see he thought he was hot stuff and the kind of rich, sophisticated, post-Yale type who is a lawyer and flies to Lake Geneva spas for skiing and goat placenta injections.

But I was still in control. I gave out more cards, pencils, and menus. I knew I'd never be able to pronounce or remember the guests' real names, which they printed on top of their room numbers, so I just kept thinking of them as look-alike celebrities so I'd have a chance to recall what was for whom. I shot Twiggy, Bella, and Harrison their appetizers, and thought I really was smart to get the whole table of ten caught up with each other. Their order blanks began to handle like a deck of cards as I fanned them out to see what the second courses would be. They were all having soup. Harrison was having *vichyssoise*, Twiggy was having *tapioca*, Bella wanted *cream of asparagus*, Dr. Brothers was having *minestrone*, the secretaries were having *soup aux herbes*, and the other four divorcée types I decided to just group together in my mind as the Four Horsewomen of the Apocalypse when they all ordered *soupe bonne femme*. I was rushing for the kitchen when I looked over my left shoulder and saw Louie seating at my table four more socialites, who looked like Aristotle Onassis, Jackie Kennedy, Sir Laurence Olivier, and Whoopi Goldberg. Aristotle Onassis turned out to be a royal pain called Mr. Micci, whose name stuck in my brain because I once had a pet boa constrictor named Micci.

Now, I want to record in my own behalf that I was performing very competently all through Mr. Micci's table's appetizers and halfway into the stag table's entrées. I was running like crazy, looking across once in a while to see if Della could see I was beginning to sweat. She looked so unearthly and calm, while the whole dining room had filled up and the band had moved in and was playing ''Some Enchanted Evening'' and ''They Call It the Jersey Bounce.'' I mean, it was really lovely. The kitchen, on the other hand, was turning into a madhouse. Waiters and waitresses, busboys and Indians, subchefs and pastry people were running into each other verbally and physically. The dining room was bubbling and suave, but the kitchen sounded like a Sing Sing prison riot. I had managed to clear the soup course and served the stags a *stuffed broiled hen,* a *chicken in cream sauce Louhans style,* a *cock in red wine,* a *rabbit,* a *venison in mustard sauce,* and one *pigeon aux petits pois.* Mr. Micci was the first one to complain on behalf of his table.

''We've been waiting a while, Eugene,'' he informed me.

''The stag table came in first.'' I smiled.

He forced a grin back, but I could see if I didn't get the entrées on his table fast there was going to be trouble. I was doing the best I could and only lost my concentration for a moment to look at Della, which is when I dropped Princess Di's chicken. That was what I think my English teacher, Miss Racinski, would have called the inciting event. It turned out to be the beginning of the end for me. It didn't take long to scoop up the poultry cadaver, but it broke my confidence. I couldn't bear to check if Della was watching me squatting between the tables shoving the carcass onto a saucer and carrying the mess to my tray stand. Seven more horrible things happened, which built to my true damnation. Louie seated a party of six who owned some major laxative company like Johanson's Milk of Magnesia or something. This table was at least twenty feet even farther away from the kitchen, and Louie asked if I could take care of it. It took me a second to realize I'd have twenty guests then, which would mean 20 × 7 = $140 dollars a week in tips, and I also didn't want Louie to think I was inept, so I said I'd love it. Then, Tina Turner wanted to change from her cock in red-wine sauce to a slab of venison. While I was serving the laxative table's appetizers, Mr. Micci informed me that he wanted a wet towel. That meant still another special trip to the kitchen. I brought the towel back with a pineapple juice, two creamed herrings, and three prune juices but forgot the lemons. Mr. Micci wiped his face with the towel and passed it to his wife, and his whole table wanted to know if there was any lemon sherbet for them to clear their palates with before trying additional entrées. The table of six all wanted fillets of sole, which meant I had to get on a line of about twelve waiters and waitresses who were waiting for Bunker to fill the orders for their tables. The flames, heat, smoke, and lines in the whole broiler section were overpowering now. Bunker was really turning the fillets out. He'd toss them in a dozen or so different frying pans then fly the ready ones onto preheated dinner plates, and another kitchen worker would slap an aluminum cover on them so they could be stacked like all the other entrées. Some waiters carried six or seven separate stacks *five high* on the same tray and marched with them through the swinging doors like charging battleships. Sweat was pouring down my face, and I knew I had fallen far behind before it was finally my turn.

"You look stuck, Snooks!" Bunker laughed hideously.

"I'm fine," I said.

"Yeah? Well, I think you're losing it."

He made sure it took as long as possible to get my order out, and when I got back to my station several of my guests were getting ugly. The stag table was screaming at me to get them their desserts and coffee. Dr. Joyce Brothers, Jill Clayburgh, and Princess Di had written down three desserts each, including *cherries jubilee,* which I was supposed to pour brandy on and light. Mr. Micci's table called Captain Pegeen to report me. Tina Turner threatened to go straight to the maître d'. The laxative people were calling me incompetent. They began to demand impossible things. Get me a toothpick. Where are our fingerbowls? Find me baking soda for the gravy you've spilled on my blouse. Crumb the table. We insist on water. Half and half! We wrote *mocha,* not *toffee.* Twenty supposedly civilized people had turned into vicious, snarling animals, and they were tearing at me. My mind became crazed and dumbfounded. I was so frightened I slipped and dropped a pot of tea, which boiled my right ankle. I was going mad, and yet my lips kept trying to be happy and my eyes kept darting to see Della to see if she saw me sinking. I now hated all my guests. I wanted to put them in a cage and sedate them with a tranquilizer machine gun. Just as I was about to completely crack, their bellyaching reached a crescendo, and I told them all I was going to the kitchen to get them everything they all wanted. They still bellowed other things after me as I hurried away with my tray. I went into the kitchen, the last shred of my sanity guiding me. It took me to the vast ice cream freezer, where the waiters and waitresses had to scoop and set up their own dessert orders. I grabbed a large supreme bowl and began shoveling big scoops of ice cream into it. Pistachio. Lime. Strawberry. Oreos and Cream. World Class Chocolate. Burnt Almond. Vanilla. It was at least a half gallon. I smothered the succulent globs with hot butterscotch, bubbling caramel, and mixed sprinkles. Then I zipped quickly by the dishwashing machine. Mahatma was the only one who noticed me. He didn't say anything, and I didn't care if he did. I grabbed an iced-tea spoon, and went down the stairs and out the zoo door into the night. I stumbled toward the lake and into the shadows that formed several hundred feet from the glare of the dining room lights. Then I circled out in front of the hotel and found a spot on a bench on the deserted, white guest dock. From there I could see the vast expanse of the spectacular hotel. It was aglow like an ocean liner stranded on a sand dune. The picture windows of the dining room were a row of enormous fish tanks. I could see the thousand creatures inside. Rich sea animals flashing, gorging. I saw my sharks and all the other moray eels and bettas and sparkling barracudas. As I trembled and slowly ate my ice cream, my eyes caught sight of the lovely Della again. She was Venus ascending, magnificently, religiously, from a clam shell. It was the Fourth of July, and she was the fireworks in my heart. That moment I knew all I had to do was figure out how I could come to possess her.

Still Friday, July 5

The next morning I was filled with shame. I thought I'd be fired the second I showed my face in the dining room, but the only one who said anything to me was Louie. "What happened to you last night?" he chuckled, and didn't even wait for an answer. It was as though nothing hideous had happened at all. Only half the stag table showed up for breakfast, two from Mr. Micci's table and only one guest from the laxative table. Less than half the guests showed up·at everyone's stations, and when I asked Scotty what was going on he told me that's the way it is all through the social season. Almost all the rich, suave persons go downstairs after dinner to the hotel nightclub for drinking and dancing their brains out. Scotty also filled me in on a few other differences between the convention routine and the social season:

1) The dining room closes for breakfast at nine-thirty, and any guests who stagger down after that go into a special Continental Breakfast room off the lobby, where they help themselves to dainty miniature cheese and prune Danishes and coffee.

2) The guests who didn't make it to the dining room are still supposed to tip twenty-five cents, which I thought was a good policy.

3) Alfredo is maître d' of the nightclub, too, and Louie assists him down there just like in the dining room.

4) Alfredo's in-group of favorite waiters work the

nightclub as well, so they really rake in the cash and give extra kickbacks. I wasn't jealous about that because I have my hands full as it is.

Della didn't show up at breakfast. Captain Pegeen, whose braids were strapped down on top of her head this morning, told me Della had permission to alternate with another waitress to cover each other's stations in the mornings since so few guests show up. Captain Pegeen told me this out near her locker in the kitchen, where she was stashing a big, white pillow she carries with her. It's just a regular personal sleeping pillow, and I asked her what she was doing with it, and she nonchalantly told me that some nights she sleeps over her bartender boyfriend's place instead of the dorm and that her head is very sensitive to what pillow it lies on. The place didn't seem as important to her as the pillow.

I noticed Bunker wasn't working the morning grill either.

After breakfast I re-set up my station for lunch and started walking to town. When I got to the bridge, there was a noise similar to a space launch, and I thought I was hallucinating again. I saw the body and face of Della flying across the top of the water about five hundred feet out on the lake. It took me a full ten countdown before I realized she was seated on the passenger side of an airboat exactly like the kind you see in the Everglades swamps. She was in some kind of combination bathing suit and diaphanous skirt ensemble, and the airplane propeller behind her decelerated from an ear-splitting roar as the boat glided toward a marina dock with a sign announcing "Buzz-Ro-All." Later on I found out three guys owned the marina—Buzz, Robert, and Allen—and they made up the name by taking the beginning of all their names. It was real hicky. By the time I got across the bridge, the boat had slowed enough for me to see Bunker sitting next to Della, steering the weird boat. I wanted to throw up, because they really looked like a physically glamorously matched couple, and my heart fell because I knew there was little chance I was going to be able to compete with that kind of hydro-excitement. Bunker was wearing a shiny, black nylon bathing suit, showing off every muscle in his arms, stomach and legs, but his eyes still had a lurking schizoid quality that made him look like a spiritual sleazeball. He still resembled Matt Dillon, but as though a paparazzo's flashbulb had just exploded in his face and the reflection was bouncing out of his corneas like a surprised cockaloony bird. But Della's streaming dark hair and smart beauty held firm against the powerful assault of the sunshine. I stopped on the bridge to watch the airboat inch the last few feet to the dock. Della started to stand and ready herself to get off. I was terrified she'd fall backward into the spinning airplane propeller. I had a horrible premonition of her being sucked into the blades and her head being chopped off, but then I could see the propeller was safely housed in a strong metal cage. That's all the boat really was. Two seats on pontoons, an airplane motor, and a cable steering gizmo that controlled a rudder behind. I really felt a very bad pain in my heart when Bunker gave Della a kiss. Della laughed and leaped onto the dock. Then Bunker turned the boat around, pushed the motor to high throttle and took off at top speed, roaring like a B-29. In a flash he was making tremendous waves and heading straight toward me on the bridge. I didn't have time to hide. He gave me a big, rotten flash of pearly whites as he headed under me and brayed "Hi, Snooks!" so loudly I could hear it over the boat's roar. The bridge vibrated, and I was hoping he'd have a nonfatal crash into one of the cement sides of the bridge, but he went straight on under and into the main channel. He headed toward a large bay to the north. It was only then I noticed there was a tank on one side of the pontoons, and a couple of squirting nozzles that shot little blasts of a yellow-green chemical into the water on each side. It was really weird.

I turned away and continued past the bridge on the road toward town. I won't say I wasn't very curious about where Della was, and I picked up my pace because I knew Buzz-Ro-All had to have a driveway somewhere nearby to get from the marina onto Skunks Misery Lane. I reached the street entrance at the precise moment Della was walking out. Her incredible dark eyebrows lay calmly above her delicate eyes as she appoached. She was looking slightly downward, as though counting cobblestones. Finally, she saw me and smiled.

"Hello," she said.

"Hi," I said. We unavoidably merged on the sidewalk and had to walk side by side. I was in awe. Her beauty was profound.

"I'm Della," she said.

"I'm Eugene Dingman," I said.

"Nice to meet you. Where're you from?"

"Bayonne."

"Where's that?"

"New Jersey."

"Oh."

"Where're you from?" I asked.

"Loudon's Landing."

"Here?"

"My whole life."

"No kidding."

"I really like it, except for a month or two in the winter when it gets cold."

I stayed curbside and as much in profile as possible, because I hate the shape of sections of my right hair.

"I thought you'd be from Florida, like most of the others," I said.

"Oh, no, I'm only sixteen. I've got another year at Loudon High before I'll be doing much traveling. You still in high school?"

"I'm just going into my senior year," I admitted. "Do you like reading books very much?"

"Yes," she said, looking at me like I was really strange.

"I'm reading *Madame Bovary* just now."

"You're kidding!" she said.

"No."

"It's *French!*" She glowed. "I love the French! I only read the French."

"No kidding!" I really felt fate had led me to her now. It was too much of a coincidence that of all the classics I brought I had started with one that was French. I just knew she was a girl who read.

"I've been mainly studying French on my own," she said, "but someday I want to work at the French Embassy or teach French. I just can't believe you're actually reading *Madame Bovary*. My mother would die if she caught me with that one. I'm really excited for you."

"You are?"

"Yes. Nobody in Loudon's Landing reads any fiction. The hotel staff only reads the Saratoga racing sheets. Of course, migrant hotel work isn't the easiest way to earn a living."

"Louie's from around here, isn't he?" I muttered. I

didn't know if I could stay conscious much longer in her beautiful presence.

"Yes, but Louie works winters at Lake Placid and Loon Lake, because they've got good ski seasons. When the hotel closes in September, the head chef and most of the others go down to Palm Beach and hotels in Daytona or Key West. You know Bunker . . . ?"

"Yes . . ." I knew she recalled Bunker's hand clamped on my neck, shoving my face into the kiwis.

"I know he's been picking on you, but he teases everybody," she consoled.

"You're his girlfriend, aren't you?"

She walked a few steps. "Not steady."

"Somebody said you were."

"My mother's from Sicily and says I'm too young for boyfriends. She thinks I should wait until I'm forty."

"Wasn't that you out with Bunker in the airboat?" I asked as though I didn't know.

"Yes. It's his. I go out with him once in a while. Last summer was my first season at the hotel, and we got to know each other. He's from Coconut Grove. His father runs a monkey menagerie, and Bunker does short order for him every winter. His father used to have a five-legged cow once, but it died. Used to be a big draw, Bunker says."

"Why's he got an airboat up here?"

"He worked out a deal with the Lake Henry Chamber of Commerce to spray weed killer in the bays."

"Doesn't it kill the fish?"

"No. He only sprays a few times a week. Usually afternoons." I could see she was bored. "Say, look, it was nice talking to you," she summed up. "I've got to go home and help my mom make calamari."

"Okay," I said.

"Congratulations on reading *Madame Bovary*."

I could tell she was dying to get away from me.

By now we had reached the point where Skunks Misery Lane meets Main Street. Della waved good-bye and began a slow run past a hardware store and a diner that boasted homemade rhubarb and peach pies à la mode. Moments later she disappeared up a street where the town sloped. All I could glimpse was a few dilapidated houses with sagging porches that looked like they had been crushed by decades of winter snow.

In town I went to the P.O. and opened a personal mailbox for fifty cents a month. I couldn't trust my correspondence reaching me directly at the hotel with a character like Mrs. Brady in charge. Then I bought a Clark bar. My father used to always bring me home Clark bars.

At lunch all Della said to me was "Hi" as she walked by with a piece of strawberry cheesecake for some lady wearing a turban.

At dinner I almost got stuck again. Mr. Micci was the only one who complained heavily, because I was slow getting him his wet towel, and Princess Di said she had ordered *veal Milanese*, not *capon*. Della didn't even look at me. Mahatma was the only one who watched me. He always looks like he's dissecting my mind.

Saturday, July 6

1) Beatrix Potter and Sylvester Stallone born 1886 and 1946, respectively.

2) Della didn't say a word to me. I can't look her in the eye. She's grown more splendiferous than ever. Much excitement in my mailbox today, which has the combination right 7, left 20, and left again to 34. In case any criminal employee snoops in this diary, they should know this combination is coded but close enough so I'll be reminded if I forget the real combination.

3) The headline in my latest *Bayonne News & Sun* is BOY GEORGE FINALLY TO NAME HIS IDEAL MAN. The news release went on to say the gender-bender is expected to confess soon he'd most like to be in love with Lee Iacocca, Michael Jackson, or the Pope. Another article on page 7 did a really fine job asking the question HAS ROCK GONE TOO FAR? I thought it very fairly discussed both sides of the debate over sex, violence, and devil worship in lyrics and videos. A third piece was very informative about dental plaque and exposed that the "typical American larder" has expanded from pizza to tempura, tofu and pita bread. Other intriguing headlines were:

A) HARVARD GRADUATES RULE AMERICA!

B) HUBBIE LEAVES HEIRESS FOR MALE STRIPPER

C) CORONER'S PET POODLE ROMPS IN MORGUE

I got a letter from Penelope:

Dear Eugene,

Dad called and wanted to meet me in a Greenwich Village deli. He didn't once mention helping me with college. He knew better than to bring his girlfriend along. He still thinks he's hot stuff in his cop uniform. He gave me a box of almond horns and a twenty-three-pound turkey he got as a bribe from a butcher. I know you like him, but I can't stand him. I never want to see him again and I told him so. Mom is smothering me. I got the job at the Bayonne dry goods store. I think of you often. Our father is a bastard. Enclosed please find five dollars. Buy a sundae with wet walnuts.

> *Love,*
> *Penelope*

I finished reading the letter and felt completely depressed. I wanted to kiss my sister for sending me the five dollars, but more than anything I wished she could forgive our father. If only she didn't hate him so much.

Sunday, July 7

1) Ringo Star born, 1940.
2) Mother Cabrini canonized, 1946.
3) Della hasn't spoken to me again. I know she's decided I'm too homely and slow-witted for her. I'm halfway through *Madame Bovary*. So far it's about a man called Charles who goes to treat the broken leg of a farmer and gets attracted to his daughter, Emma, who has black hair, brown eyes, and full lips. Emma's a good wife but finds her husband boring, and she goes to a

ball. Then she finds she has a lot in common with a clerk—they share an interest in music, poetry, and discussions about the dullness of small towns. She has a baby, and she finds that's a bore. She frets. She mopes. Then she makes love with a man of brutal temperament called Rodolphe as they listen to speeches at an agricultural show. Then Emma decides to study music again.

Last night I had my second wet dream.

I collected my tip envelopes today. I've made $97.27. It's too complicated for me to figure out who cheated me, but I think it was the Four Horsewomen of the Apocalypse or Harrison Ford. I'll keep closer tabs during my second week.

Monday, July 8

1) Reverend Jesse Jackson, American religious leader, born in 1941.

2) In Massachusetts it is illegal to eat peanuts in church or use tomatoes in clam chowder.

3) I went to town and opened a savings account at the First National Bank of Loudon's Landing.

4) Received an oversized postcard from Mom showing a picture of the Golden Nugget Casino in Atlantic City:

Dear Eugene,

Mr. Mayo bought a used Packard car in mint condition and took me for a little blackjack to celebrate. How are the mountains? I've lost five and three-quarters pounds at the Swift Diet Center. Mr. Mayo has moved up from the cellar and is sleeping in your room until September when the hotel closes and you come home. I made a great ravioli with NutraSweet. I love Passages. *I've completely forgotten about your throwing the spoon at my leg. Penelope's getting very cranky.*

Kisses to you and best wishes from Mr. Mayo. Drink your O.J.!

Mom

Tuesday, July 9

1) Doughnut cutter patented, 1872.

2) Today at breakfast Alfredo told me Mr. Micci's table and the laxatives' table are full-season guests. That means they'll be with me to the end—right through Labor Day. Mr. Micci acts more and more like a living memorial to Aristotle Onassis. He orders four of everything on the menu. His wife is the one who looks like Jackie Kennedy, and the other look-alike couple with them—Sir Laurence Olivier and Whoopi Goldberg—talk a mile a minute about provocative things like the Republican Party and herpes as a Communist plot. I've had a chance to focus in on the laxative company's owner and the five other members of his family at his table. The owner's name is Philip Van der Kamp—King Ex-Lax. His wife I think of as Queen Ex-Lax. The other four I've dubbed Uncle Ex-Lax, Aunt Ex-Lax, Sissy Ex-Lax and Sonny Ex-Lax. I don't think Sonny is anybody's real son at the table. He looks and acts like a handsome female impersonator in a young man's suit.

The table's very weird, as though they've participated in too much inbreeding or backgammon.

My stag table almost completely changed at Sunday's check-out. Everyone except the Harrison Ford, the Dr. Joyce Brothers, the Bella Abzug, and the Twiggy look-alikes checked out, but the new guests I got looked and acted just like the others, so I still have Princess Di, Jacqueline Bisset, Jill Clayburgh, and Tina Turner types. They're different people, but they're still the Four Horse-women of the Apocalypse to me. The only main change was the two desperate secretary types were changed to two men, which thrilled all the girls. These men are just as educated and smooth-looking as Harrison, but their heads look more like Arnold Schwarzenegger's and a Brat Packer's. I don't care. I still have twenty paying customers, and this Sunday I'll open their tip envelopes as they give them to me to make sure none of them stiffs or shortchanges me.

I now avoid Della completely. I'm intimidated by both her beauty and her French-trained brain. I can see she's brilliant. Today by accident I went through the swinging doors right after her and I smelled a faint trace of lavender scent. I was thrilled. I bet my father once felt the same way when he smelled my mother's per-fume. You're all I have, Dear Diary, and I'm learning to cherish you more each day. You're turning out to be a wonderful, dependable friend. There's still so much I need to confess. I can feel myself being able to reach deeper into my soul than any living person will let me, except maybe Penelope. I finished *Madame Bovary*. She was lonely too. If she'd kept a good diary or journal she wouldn't have had to lie so much. If you ask me, she had a lot of sex but no love at all. She didn't know how to love. And she didn't hold down an honest job. It wasn't her fault. She didn't have *Ms.* magazine or transactional analysis to help her back in the 1800s. I felt moisture on my eyeballs when she ate the handful of arsenic at the end. She dies in agony and her husband is prostrated, not to mention broke. If Della reads *Madame Bovary* I bet she wouldn't go out with Bunker. I saw them on the airboat again this morning. I am frustrated. Miserable. I want to be a genius. Every day I'll record and learn at least two or three items from the following list of what I consider to be steps toward becoming an intellectual:

1) Read at least two chapters of a literary work of art.

2) Look up a vocabulary word I don't know.

3) Find and memorize a new historical fact.

4) Research an important date from history.

5) Answer correspondence and write a letter, but record a copy of it for my old-age memoirs.

6) Possibly write a short story or poem and send it to the *Atlantic Monthly* or the *New Jersey Literary Review*.

7) Record and analyze my dreams.

8) Have a new philosophic thought.

9) Remember a famous person who was born or died, from my *Famous Births and Deaths* book.

10) Read a myth.

11) Jot down a self-improvement fact.

12) Read about obscure customs.

13) Learn French.

14) Learn Latin.

15) Add to these steps any new steps I deem necessary.

16) Read the *Bayonne News & Sun* and *The Loudon's Landing Gazette* every day. Record mind-boggling headlines and summarize.

My new vocabulary word for today is:

ter•gi•ver•sa•tion (tûr ´ji-vər-sā ´shən) *n*. The action of turning one's back on; i.e., abandonment of a cause. This word does not apply to my father.

Wednesday, July 10

a) *Bayonne News & Sun*—BIGFOOT TEENAGER HAS 22-INCH TOOTSIES!

b) Author Marcel Proust born, 1871—he was asthmatic.

c) Princess Elizabeth and Philip Mountbatten engaged, 1947.

d) Sent brief responses to Mom and Penelope on guest stationery with a letterhead showing beautiful Lake Henry and the hotel. Much fancier writing paper than Holiday Inn's. Longer letters to come, I told them. Sent $25 to Penelope as surprise.

e) I'm still sick over Della. The mere sight of her paralyzes me. I feel totally inadequate near her.

f) Have begun reading *Crime and Punishment* by Fyodor Dostoyevsky.

g) I must write to my father. I know he could advise me. I think I need him very much now.

Mahatma invited me to come see him at the "Indian House" tonight. I told him I couldn't make it. He made a little circle gesture in the air. "Love and a cough cannot be hid," he whispered! At first I decided he didn't really say that, but I couldn't have imagined such a freaky sequence of words. It annoyed me. I had no intention of going to his "Indian House," whatever that was.

Della served a chilled oyster cocktail across the aisle from me and could have very easily given me a little wave. She didn't. After Mahatma had dropped his Bombay bon mot I couldn't even look at *him* anymore. I finished setting up and slipped down a staircase near the chef's glass booth. I got out of the hotel and made it back through the night to my room. I put on my pj's and read until Dostoyevsky has Rodian Romanovitch Raskolnikov, familiarly called Rodya, fork over his watch to a 60-year-old, slovenly lady pawnbroker, and his sister Dunya loses her job as governess in the family of Svidrigaylov and decides to marry a middle-aged lawyer. By 11 P.M. I was so depressed I got dressed and found Mrs. Brady in her fright wig.

"Why do the Indians have a separate house?" I asked.

"Because they cook with too much curry!" she said, then told me where "Indian House" was. It turned out to be right near the bridge and down at the edge of the lake.

The Indian House was white with two floors like a cheap Cape Cod shack, but in better shape than the employees' ex-turkey coop. It also had nice lighting outside and a screen door that let me see in the minute I stepped up to the front. Inside looked dark, but I could make out a lot of brown bodies moving around like graceful zombies. I knocked on the door and Mahatma emerged from the shadows. He looked amused to see me, saying, "Hello, come in." His voice was squeaky and abrupt as usual, with an accent like I had heard only twice before. Once was in the movie *Gandhi* and the other time was when I took a gypsy cab in Bayonne and got an elderly driver from Barbados who was a Seventh-Day Adventist.

I stepped inside and saw a big room all lit by candles. The whole Indian work crew drifted over to greet me with bows. This including Buddhakariskaman and Buddhafatima and eight or so others who all looked like Sabu and sounded like they had the same name. They were in their usual bright shirts and robes and shorts, and they were busily chopping onions and cubing meats and cooking in what looked like a tandoori oven. The smell of curry hit me like a sonic boom. My head was knocked back and my nostrils dilated like a Hottentot's waist. I could smell the stuff through my ears. Then I saw what looked like eighty chicken thighs stacked on a plate and a gross of gizzards frying away in a wok.

Mahatma took me to one of the dozens of pillows on the floor that looked like they had been purchased at a harem garage sale.

"We cook all our own food here," he explained. We sat down and Buddhakariskaman pushed a plate into my hands.

"You don't eat at the zoo?"

"No. We like spicier and better food. The hotel gives us what we want. You like curried chicken?"

"No . . ."

"Try it."

In a flash my plate was flooded with four thighs and a mound of white rice. Mahatma noshed away from his own platter. Everybody was laughing and smiling, not *at* me, just good-naturedly and in lieu of conversation since they probably suspected I didn't know how to eat Indian style. They were picking everything up with their fingers.

"Eat! Eat!" Mahatma urged, with everyone grinning.

I didn't want to hurt their feelings. I picked up a morsel of chicken and took the smallest bite I could. A blast of renegade paprika rushed along my tongue and crashed up into my sinuses. It felt like I had slurped a combination of Chinese hot mustard and pulverized pepperoni.

"It's delicious," I remarked, thinking my nose was knocked onto the top of my head. My eyes, though moist, had gotten accustomed to the candlelight, and I looked around the room to drink in more of its detail while downing a glass of water. They had one rather large statue with three eyes, and music playing with pretty cymbals. I noticed lots of tapestries and even a warrior statue made of wood. The whole thing was very religious-looking and oriental. There was a special writing desk set on the floor and I noticed a lot more watercolor paintings with images like the Indians wore on their shirts and robes. What the room looked most like was as though Mahatma had made one of his circular hand gestures and an eclectic Sri Lankan interior decorator had gone crazy.

"You guys Buddhists?" I asked.

"Some of us. I'm Hindu—not orthodox," Mahatma said. "A few others are Sikhs, Jains and Lingayats. We're like a religious smorgasbord here."

"That's nice," I said, and made some other small talk while the gizzard course was served.

"You all go to Miami in September?"

"No. Detroit."

"Detroit?"

"Winters we usually work for General Motors. Sometimes Chrysler. Once or twice we've worked on the Ford assembly line. We're only doing kitchen work during the summers here. The rest of the year we work with hot steel and welding."

"No kidding?"

"We have a biological talent, you know. We can stand heat. Indians are very much in demand in the United States for such work. Americans are not used to heat. India is a very hot place, so we're used to it."

"That's why you run the glassware machines and do the pots?"

"Yes. We get paid very well," Mahatma said. "We always get our own house. Our own food. Our own clothing. We get anything we want, because nobody wants our jobs. We're also unionized."

I looked at the Indian men sitting near all those lit candles.

"We have a good life. Lake Henry Hotel, Mercury, T-Bird corporations are afraid to fire us because nobody enjoys one-hundred-five-degrees Fahrenheit labor. We're originally from the Bengal jungles where it's as hot as hell."

"You like your jobs?"

" 'If it's too hot in the kitchen, then get out!' President Truman said that when he retired," Mahatma chuckled, and the others giggled with him. I don't think they had the faintest idea of what he said.

"Did Truman say, 'Love and a cough cannot be hid,' too?" I asked.

Mahatma smiled at me. He turned his back to the others and lowered his voice. "No. *I* mostly say that. I said that to you because you look like you're ready to walk into the lake and drown yourself!"

I wanted to tell him to mind his own business, but I caught sight of myself in a mirror with an ornate, enameled frame depicting devils. I was sitting with my chest collapsed, my neck craned forward, and peering sideways out of the corner of my eye. I looked like an introverted idiot.

"Why do you care about me?" I whispered.

"Because I know you're not an animal like most of the others at this hotel. You're too young to be with evil people."

"I can take care of myself," I said, my voice a bit shaky.

"You're defensive now," Mahatma said. "I can also see you're two other things. You're attracted to the beautiful waitress with the ponytail, and you're frightened of Bunker at the grill. You're as scared as a baboon running from a tiger. Buddha said when someone does not have a friend, then *we* must be that friend."

I couldn't speak for a moment. I just looked into the old man's eyes, which had a lot of capillaries but a clear blue light in the centers. "I don't know who Buddha is," I faintly admitted, "except I read once he sat under a tree for a long time and thought a lot."

"It's not important for you to know who Buddha is. Or who any of our Indian gods are. You'll find out when you want. Never, maybe."

I thought maybe he had just been leading up to handing me a couple of *The Watchtower* Jehovah's Witnesses pamphlets.

"I told you I'm not orthodox. You came tonight because you *needed* to."

"I didn't know that," I protested. "I thought I came because you invited me."

"There's nothing wrong with need."

He looked genuinely concerned about me.

"Your eyes are red. It's okay to cry here," Mahatma

told me. He helped me up from the floor and led me away from the others. Soon we were standing alone in front of the statue with three eyes.

"My eyes are red from your tasty chicken," I told him.

"You want to cry," he said.

I just looked at the third eye, which seemed to be a big, purple piece of cut glass.

"You're in pain, young man. Here at our Indian House it's quite all right to suffer. And do you know why you hurt? I'll tell you. You're a watcher, not a doer. You must learn to do."

"How?"

"You need to know many secrets. You need to know the answers to many mysteries. That's why you came here tonight. I will teach you what you need to know. I'll be your friend."

"Why would you want to be my friend?"

He made one of his circle gestures in the air, and then stung me by saying, "Because you have no father."

I felt suddenly nervous, even afraid. "You don't know anything about me."

"I can tell when a boy has no father."

Mahatma put his hand on my shoulder. He touched me like an ancient grandfather. I didn't say anything. My fear melted and I felt a rush of memories.

"This is Shiva," Mahatma introduced me to the statue. "With his three eyes he is boundless and powerful, spectacular in energy. He is Time, Justice, Water, Sun, Destroyer and Creator."

"That's nice."

"Sometimes he has five heads, ten hands and his middle eye is shaped like a crescent. His throat is dark blue. His hair is fine red. His hair projects like a horn from his forehead.''

I began to lean closer, watching Mahatma's wrinkled old hand point out protrusions from the shadows.

"He wears a garland of shells carved like human skulls," Mahatma continued, "and a second necklace of serpents. He holds a trident. Notice Shiva's body is covered with vipers, which represents immortality. Everything about him is circular, round. Shiva is the secret of Life," Mahatma said. Then he made another whirling gesture, this time more slowly, like he was trying to hypnotize me.

I looked at Shiva's purple third eye, and I felt I was beginning to grow one in the middle of my own forehead. Maybe I was destined to grow a third eye that would see things I could only dare write in this secret journal. Then visions danced into my head about death. I saw my mom for a moment. And Miss Elena Racinski. And my father taking me fishing when I was eight. I saw a Snickers bar. I saw an island. I remembered animal eyes staring at me. Mahatma was someone special. I felt we had a lot in common. A Bayonne boy and an unorthodox, elderly Hindu. I heard voices. Echoes. Maybe from other lives. Buddhakariskaman and Buddhafatima. Captain Pegeen and Alfredo. I felt on the verge of knowing fantastic things. I did want to cry. Instead I just sat down on a pillow in front of Shiva and told Mahatma the story of my life. When I had finished, Mahatma told me there was something very holy Shiva would really want me to do.

"What?" I wanted to know.

"Ask Della for a date," he said.

Thursday, July 11

1) Exactly three months ago today my mother's lover moved into our cellar.

2) The ghost ship of Doom—The Flying Dutchman—was sighted today at 4 A.M., 1881.

3) "It doesn't matter what you do in the bedroom, as long as you don't do it in the street and frighten the horses."—Mrs. Patrick Campbell

4) Della worked breakfast. She looked particularly brilliant and sensitive near her station's picture window. I asked her if I could walk her home after the meal. She said no. It was a nice no. Not rude. Actually she looked surprised. She explained she had a previous commitment to go spraying with Bunker.

Friday, July 12

1) Kirsten Flagstad born, 1895.

2) Asked Della if she'd like to go for a swim off the employees' dock after lunch. She said no.

Saturday, July 13

1) Marat stabbed in his bathtub, 1793.

2) Asked Della if she had time to have a Coke. She said no. She said she had to go home and help her mother make spaghetti. I waited until Mahatma was busy with pots before I brought my dirty dishes out. Anytime he even looks at me now he seems to be asking something.

Sunday, July 14

1) Isaac Bashevis Singer born, 1904.

2) Raked in one hundred and twelve dollars and twenty-five cents today. I've narrowed the stiffer down to someone at Mr. Micci's table. Asked Della out. She said no. I told Mahatma. "Keep trying," he advised. I thought he was going to give me some great secret pointers.

Monday, July 15

1) Robert Pershing Wadlow—the world's tallest man—died in 1940. He was 8 feet, 11 inches, and twenty-two years old. A foot disease.

2) Billy the Kid killed by Sheriff Pat Garrett, 1881.

3) Made deposit at First National Bank of Loudon's Landing.

4) Extra depressed. Finally read back issues of *Bayonne News & Sun*. Highlights were articles called WHAT WOMEN SECRETLY WANT FROM LOVE; PRISCILLA PRESLEY ROCKS *DALLAS* SET; and LIBYAN LOONY HAS PRICE ON HIS HONKER.

5) I checked on more specific places to take Della on date:

   a) The Loudon's Landing Cinema is playing an unromantic oldie called *The Thing*. The only performances are on Thurs., Fri. and Sat. nights at 8 & 11 P.M.

   b) Hairy Mary's Place serves pizza.

   c) Ride on the Lake Henry Excursion Boat. Two hours. See Fort Lake Henry, including Revolutionary War Museum. $7.50 per person, complete package.

   d) Sunbathe at public beach at the foot of Mohawk Street.

   e) Clara & Flo's Algonquin Soda Shoppe.

6) I asked Della out. She said no. She looks worried when I come near her. I'm ready to give up.

7) Thought about writing to my best friend, Calvin Kennedy, in Bayonne, but I'm really still offended for his lying to me about being sick with 104° fever.

Tuesday, July 16

1) Asked Della out. She said no.
2) Received letter from Mom:

Dear Eugene,

I don't know quite how to tell you, but Mr. Mayo and I have fallen in love. I gave it a lot of thought and decided I'd just better let you know. I've done very well at the diet center. I've discovered if I put Light 'n Lively low-fat cottage cheese into the blender it comes out tasting like whipped cream. It's been my salvation. That, together with the Wasa crackers! Penelope doesn't approve of Mr. Mayo and me being in love, but I am most worried about your reaction. You know I haven't had romantic feelings for any man since your father took off with his New York woman. It's very hard for me to tell you about this, but my love for Mr. Mayo is very sincere. He adores sleeping in your room. We do nothing in the house that Penelope wouldn't approve of, and certainly not in your bed. I feel great admiration for Mr. Mayo, because he has overcome a very tragic childhood. His father made him kill cows, so he can't eat steak. We go to drive-ins in the Packard, and we really enjoy wrestling. I think Mr. Mayo used to work for the Mafia, but we don't talk about that since he's quite retired and limps like he does. I can thank Gail Sheehy and Passages *that I've found love once more. I also think I was partly at fault in your father going astray and our divorce. How are the mountains? I hope you're making loot. I'm thinking of reading Shirley MacLaine's new book, but my diet counselor thinks she sings and does high kicks better than writing. I feel happier now that I've expressed myself about me and Mr. Mayo. Have a nice day.*

Kisses to you and "ciao" from Charlie.

Mom

Wednesday, July 17

1) "Not to go to the theater is like making one's toilet without a mirror."—Schopenhauer

2) I asked Della out. She said no. I asked Mahatma what I should do. He said, "Keep asking her. Try a canoe ride." I think there's too many mysteries I need answers to. Mahatma's inscrutable.

Thursday, July 18

1) Teddy drove off bridge at Chappaquiddick, 1969.

2) After breakfast I went to Buzz-Ro-All. Got list of prices:

Motor Boats

    5 horsepower = $10 an hour/$35 all day; $50 deposit

    15 hp = $20 an hour/$100 all day; $150 deposit

25 hp = $25 an hour/$125 all day; $200 deposit
Inboards only by special arrangement with managers.

Sailboats
$12 an hour/$40 all day; $75 deposit

Canoes
$3 an hour/$10 all day; $20 deposit
Water-ski rentals only by special arrangement with managers. Minimum three in boat.

Rented a canoe and took a practice cruise after lunch. Difficult to paddle and steer when there's only one person in the canoe. I understand why the expression "paddle your own canoe" is so meaningful. A dock boy showed me how to lift my paddle forward, then pull it backward while at the same time twisting it slightly to keep the bow going straight. It's a lot of work. No chance to look at the scenery.

Friday, July 19

1) Lizzie Borden and Mussolini born, 1860 and 1883 respectively.

2) Asked Della in the zoo if she wanted to go for a canoe ride. She said no. I feel terrible.

3) Asked Della by the egg timer if she wanted to go for a canoe ride. She said no.

4) Decided Mr. Micci is definitely the one stiffing me. I rethought last week's envelopes very carefully. He's supposed to tip me fourteen dollars for him and his

wife, and he puts in only ten single bills. He still orders a wet towel at every meal. I don't have enough nerve to say anything to him, but one of these days I might.

5) Bunker called me "Snooks" again and laughed at me like he knew I was constantly asking Della out. I went straight into the dining room and asked Della if she'd like to go for a canoe ride, and she was much nicer and said she had to go home and help her mother make scungilli.

6) Went to Loudon's Landing's public library. It's in a converted one-room schoolhouse. The librarian is nice and cultured. She had a book called *The Mysteries of Teenage Loving* by Dr. Louis Mudd. Because it was a research book I couldn't check it out, but I outlined its salient points:

a) The first thing that strikes one teenager about another teenager is physical appearance.

b) A teenager can forgive a boy or girl for being ugly, but he or she doesn't forget it.

c) Ugly teenage boys think girls really like them to have muscular arms, but that's false.

d) A boy who just *likes* a girl would think, "I would vote for her in a class election."

e) A boy who *loves* a girl thinks, "I would climb the World Trade Center for her."

f) The evolutionary significance of sexual attraction begins with observing elodea plants.

g) Pheromones are strange and fascinating body chemicals that create maddening scents.

h) Signals that a teenage girl doesn't like a teenage boy are:

I) She frequently looks at ceiling.

II) She gives "refrigerator stares."

III) She chain-smokes.
IV) She picks her teeth.
 V) She cracks her knuckles.
VI) She plays with split ends.

   i) Teenage boys and girls find loving difficult if either one of them has extremely negative feelings, such as depression, anxiety, loneliness, hallucinations, or crippling shyness.

I am really depressed.

10 P.M.

Finished *Crime and Punishment* by Fyodor Dostoyevsky. Good book. Really shows how a criminal is compelled to return to the scene of his crime. Have now started *The Last of the Mohicans* by James Fenimore Cooper. It's not French. Decided to write my father. Here is text:

Dear Dad:
   How is everything in NoHo? I hope you and Laurette are fine and still going up to Ray's Pizza for their delicious slices. Whenever I need to think of something fun I remember the time you and Laurette took me. I hope I didn't order too many pieces. I remember I had four, and you and Laurette only had one each. Penelope told me she saw you, so I assume she brought you up to date on my summer employment. I'm doing fine. The mountains and lake are beautiful. I've been saving my money every week, and I'd like to invite you and

Laurette to come up and visit me. I'd really like to see you both. I miss you a lot, and I've learned several water sports. I haven't seen you in over two years. I hope I didn't do anything to offend you or Laurette. Maybe you called the house and Mom didn't tell me. You know how she is, but she sounds more mellow now. I don't think she'd hang up if you called for me anymore. Of course, I'm sensitive to the fact that Laurette probably doesn't enjoy your phoning your ex-wife's residence, particularly since Mom used to scream those curses about her into the receiver. You'd laugh if you knew the things I remember now while I'm doing my aquatic endeavors. I remember things from when I was three years old and you first became a cop instead of working in your father and mother's bakery. I'm still very sad how they both died from diabetes. What I remember most is when you'd take me and Penelope out in the 32-foot skiff you had, and we'd catch porgies and rock bass off Sandy Hook. I also remember how you'd take us down to Hylan Boulevard every Sunday to where the Good Humor truck would park and buy us Cream-Sicles. You'd be surprised about all the things I remember. The time you took me to target practice, and how we'd always stop at the bridge in Prince's Bay, where the man had the giant pet sea turtle with a chain through its shell. Remember the African cockroach exhibit at the zoo? The buttery lobsters at the Beach Shanty? The horseshoe crabs? The time I was scared on the ferris wheel at Coney Island? I wouldn't be scared anymore. I've really grown up a lot and I'd really like to see you. You know you'll always be my dad no matter what you do, and I'll always be your son. Very best wishes to Laurette, and when you both get your next slice, think of me. Hope you'll write soon. Please come up and see me. I'll pay for everything. Make sure you tell Laurette I send her my best wishes and would like to see her, too. I'm glad you've both found happiness.

Your loving son,
Eugene

P.S. *I'm not just a bookworm anymore and just writing crazy stories and getting good marks. I think you'd like me now. Hi, again, Laurette. I'll put you both up at the Pine Knoll Motel. It's very plush.*

Midnight

1) I may snub Della. I think I'll dislike her soon. Am still shaken by *The Mysteries of Teenage Loving*. Maybe Mahatma knows better secrets.

2) Finally able to answer my mother's letter. Here is text:

Dear Mom:
Received your letter. I really don't like Mr. Mayo sleeping in my bed. If he has any kind of disease it could go into the mattress. Am glad you've found a way to enjoy cottage cheese. I'm worried about your suspicions of Mr. Mayo's previous "black hand" involvement. Don't sit near lighted windows, and be alert in the Packard. Enclosed please find my copy of Madame Bovary *by Gustave Flaubert. Please read it. I'm too disturbed to write any more just now.*

Love,
Eugene

P.S. *I still have one Snickers left and will think of you when I eat it.*

Saturday, July 20

1) Diana Rigg and Natalie Wood born, 1938.

2) I happened to be at the kitchen bakery depot this morning picking up an order of prune Danish and English muffins. Della came along with her tray and said hi, then ordered four slices of buttered rye and a bagel with cream cheese from Zola, the pastry chef, who is French-Canadian and has a very short brow. I asked Della if she wanted to go for a canoe ride in the afternoon, and she said yes. I didn't tell Mahatma.

3) 2 P.M., at Buzz-Ro-All. I knew she'd be a no-show. By 2:10 I had rented the canoe and was sitting in it at the end of the dock rearranging my legs and towel so I'd look less puny. My bathing trunks are black Jantzens, and I was wearing a short-sleeved, navy-blue terry-cloth shirt that wouldn't show perspiration or suntan-oil stains. I also managed to buy a pair of Mexican sunglasses at the hotel sundries store. They gave me a mysterious image but little confidence. I kept checking my reflection in a dockside chrome gas pump to be sure I looked stupid. I did. By then I felt bad that I didn't tell Mahatma. One of the secrets he knows might have been about this rejection.

2:13 P.M.

Della rushed down onto the dock saying she was really sorry but Alfredo had asked her to sign up for the employees' amateur shows, which are going to be every Wednesday night for the rest of the season. She said she had participated last year and sang "La Vie en Rose," but this year she was going to perform "What's the Use of Wonderin' " from *Carousel* and "My Heart Belongs to Daddy." She took off her sandals and Loudon High sweatshirt and in a flash got in the front, and we started paddling. She was wearing her lovely white bathing suit. She was so tastefully gorgeous, and she was in *my* canoe. I thought I was going to lose consciousness again. I was thankful she had to face forward in the bow with me in the stern, because my ankles were shaking. The enchantment that had gripped me when I'd first seen her returned with full impact. She was even more otherworldly now. I should have known then it would all end in a terrible disaster and my near death.

"Let's head for Blue Mountain Bay," she called back.

"Okay."

"Have you seen the hotel from the lake yet?"

"No," I said.

She signaled for us to go around the right side of the island. Up to now I had never ventured very far from the dock, and I was surprised at the difference in the water when we reached the open stretch of Lake Henry. I had studied a mimeographed map they pass out at

Buzz-Ro-All and knew the lake was about twenty miles long and three miles wide. The water became stark blue, and there were waves a half foot high. The canoe bounced, and Della's long hair snapped behind her. She'd turn her head from time to time, and she looked like she was having as much fun as in any airboat. She could really paddle, and together we kept up a good pace.

In a short time we came around the island at a point where the entire hotel could be seen.

"Isn't it incredible!" she called over the rush of wind and slapping of waves.

"Yes!" I shouted back.

"I love it out here! I always have!" she cried out happily.

I bubbled with so many sensations at once. I was in a kaleidoscope, a hologram. Stereophonic sound! I was overwhelmed. There was the vastness of the lake flooding out in all directions and winding its way between dozens of mountains, which stood like giants, watching. There were two islands to the south, mounds lifting out of the water with shafts of pine trees, some more than a hundred feet tall. There was the great hotel on its own island, with the annexes reaching out and clinging like white gingerbread from another century. To the far north was Blue Mountain with its bay, and the fork where the rest of the lake snaked to the right and rushed up to form a labyrinth among cliffs and smaller islands. It was primeval. No lakeside homes or other violations could be seen along the entire east and north shorelines. The water now became night blue with small, fizzling whitecaps, and here and there was a cat's-paw of wind ripples. The greens near the high mountain slopes were ever-changing shadows from the inching sun. Light, then dark emerald. And the sky was a tremendous slab of electric blue rolling high over everything. Darker blues and a purple haze danced far away over the most northern mountains, but these could only be noticed like secrets, something waiting. It was all a Technicolor dream, and I was in this extravaganza with the most pulchritudinous girl in the world. Little did I know the whole thing was going to end in a nightmare.

Water sprayed across my face. The sun etched everything with the sharpness of a razor. Its rays flowed hot into my skin. By now Della and I paddled in complete unison. It seemed to me we were one force. A part of everything. Nature was so raw it was in control. And in the middle of all this breathtaking beauty I was afraid. It took two forms. I thought about drowning. I'm a fair swimmer, but not Greystoke, the legend of Tarzan. I think the main fear came from my feeling that Bunker was hiding somewhere along the shoreline with a deer rifle and had me in the crosshairs of its telescopic sight. I also fantasized a storm would suddenly blow up and we'd capsize. While clinging to the overturned canoe I'd be eaten alive by a sturgeon. As things ended up, I wasn't very far wrong.

A half hour later we had made it to the mouth of Blue Mountain Bay. There was a complete transition in the lake's mood once we had passed behind the left thrust of land forming the bay. The wind was blocked, and the water calmed to a mirror. We stayed close to the right bank. A beaver swam nearby, then slapped its tail and dove under. Turtles dotted the surface of fallen logs along the shore. Silver fish jumped at dragonflies.

"Let's just drift," Della suggested.

"Okay," I agreed.

We put our paddles in, and Della turned around to

face me. She relaxed with her left leg hanging demurely over the side of the canoe. I was thankful my ankles had stopped shaking, and I tried to drape myself in the stern so I'd look nonchalant. We floated in silence for a while. I just couldn't say anything and wished I could ask Mahatma for a few pointers.

"I'm glad you kept asking me to do something," she finally said.

"So am I," my voice cracked.

"You must have thought I was really a snob."

"No."

"My mother was working me over."

"Is she really from Sicily?"

"*Is* she! She's very strict and constantly wants to know what I'm doing. We're just on completely different wavelengths now, and I'd like to have a rest from her. Between her and Bunker I think I'll go crazy."

"What's Bunker doing?" I muttered, not wanting to sound too interested.

"He acts like he owns me," she said. Whenever she said anything she seemed to be profoundly caught up in her thoughts. "He's really got a lot of problems of his own. The only reason I've gone out with him as much as I have is he's got the saving grace of knowing he's mixed up. All last summer we did nothing but talk about him. He's very narcissistic. You wouldn't think an assistant broiler chef could be narcissistic. He says he can date any Miami Eastern Airlines hostess he wants. And he talks about steroids and weird mushrooms and things. He says he tried the Marines, and was put in jail after his blood tests and given a dishonorable discharge."

"Do you have any things in common?" I asked.

"No. Not really. He hates to see me reading a book.

And his logic is so strange I just don't want to be exposed to it much more. I want to talk about French culture and writers like Simone de Beauvoir and Jean-Paul Sartre. He's not interested. He's not even interested in who I really am. The only foreign words he knows are à la carte. He curses a lot too, and I'm not comfortable with that."

About then, I thought I heard the sound of Bunker's airboat, and scanned the horizon but couldn't see it anywhere. I decided I was just imagining it, but I did remember Della had said he usually does his spraying in the afternoons.

At that moment, Della signaled me not to speak, and pointed. It took a moment before I could see three deer staring at us. One was a fawn with eyes just like Della's. The animals were frozen like statues. Proud. Unafraid. One buck had a great set of antlers. Finally we drifted past them.

"Have you ever read Simone de Beauvoir or Jean-Paul Sartre?' she asked.

"No," I answered, feeling deeply ignorant. "But I did finish *Madame Bovary*."

"How was it?"

"Very good."

"If only I'd been born in Paris or Nice," she sighed.

I was really beginning to wonder where her obsession with French things had come from. "Is your father French?" I asked.

"No, he's dead," she said. "He was English. But he was killed in Vietnam when I was very young. I don't really remember him. My mother keeps a picture of him on our piano. He was very handsome."

"If your mother's Sicilian and your father was English, how did you become so French?"

"My aunt Claire. She's my mother's younger sister. She's always studied French and lived in the city."

"New York?"

"Albany," she corrected.

"That's nice."

"My mother tried to keep her trapped in the Adirondacks too, but she escaped. She eloped with a man who writes dictionaries. She met him at a bar in town. He was just passing through from Montreal and they struck up a conversation. The same night she met him she went home, packed and left—with my mother screaming. At first they lived only in Albany, but he went on to do French dictionaries and Russian ones, and so they started to travel to do research in Paris and Moscow, but they kept their condo in Albany. Everything I know about the outside world I can thank my aunt Claire for. By the time I was twelve my mother had forgiven her and used to let me visit Albany once in a while. Sometimes her husband would go away on a trip alone, and I'd go down and keep Claire company. She is very colorful. She used to keep a mountain lion in her apartment."

"A real one?"

"Yes. She found it as a cub near Schroon Lake. In Albany, it grew up and she'd take it out for a walk on a leash. One year she made a matching oufit for herself out of Leatherette, and traffic would come to a halt. Crowds would gather around her and the lion. On rainy days the lion learned how to exercise in the apartment. It would leap from wall to wall and at night let out great shrieks. Neighbors started to complain, of course."

"Does she still have it?"

"No. It's dead."

"What happened?"

"The police made her give it to the Metropolitan Zoo. But it wouldn't eat, and so she had to take a bus and go downtown and feed it chopped meat herself every day."

"How did it die?"

"Andrei, her husband, got a contract to do a Swedish dictionary in Stockholm. He wanted my aunt to go, and she couldn't let the mountain lion stop her. She decided eventually the lion would get hungry enough and eat from someone else's hand. But it didn't. By the time she came back it had starved itself to death."

"That's horrible."

"My aunt was heartbroken. But there was nothing else she could do. She couldn't stop her life."

"No. And so she's the one who's influenced you more than your own mother and father?"

"Yes. She did all the things my mother should have done. She was the first one to talk to me about menstruation. She taught me how to put on makeup. France was her favorite country, and so she told me about every restaurant and street she visited there. She learned French and Russian. She and Andrei are the closest ones I know to Simone de Beauvoir and Jean-Paul Sartre. Aunt Claire's never been rich. Everything we've ever done together has been in Albany. She taught me how to buy clothes from recycle shops like Encore and MiLady Again. She helped me find Diors and other designer clothes that had been traded in by state senators' wives. She taught me how to make French sauces and stews from Provence. She taught me how to grow my own tomatoes. She helped me learn and practice French. There is a certain *je ne sais quoi* to Paris that Loudon's Landing doesn't have. And she showed me how to be selfish. Selfish in the best sense. That's how we all begin to find out who we really are, don't you think?''

She was so sophisticated I was overwhelmed. I also got the impression she was a bit ashamed of her mother for being Sicilian.

"We'd better head back," Della said.

"Oh, yes," I agreed. It *was* getting late, but I hadn't gotten around to telling her my deepest feelings for her. I had such unrealistic urges as she swung her legs back around to face front in the bow.

I considered making a sudden move and kissing her back passionately but was afraid the canoe might turn over.

I thought about lowering the center of gravity of the canoe by dropping slowly to my knees and hugging her waist. I even opened my mouth and tried to think of a way to tell her how I felt.

Before I could do anything she had started paddling, and I did likewise. We turned the canoe. Once we had left the bay and hit the main stretch of the lake, the wind and wave slaps were so loud I couldn't think of anything sensible. I was filled with dreams and expectations. My fantasies got more and more dramatic until something happened that jolted me awake:

I *really* heard Bunker's airboat.

I knew Della could hear it too, because her back stiffened. We couldn't see anything, but we were paddling down the channel between the hotel island and the next closest island. The nearest landing point was the employees' dock, which was an old, wooden platform bobbing at the bottom of a long flight of rickety stairs. About twenty of the staff were sunbathing and rubbing oils on themselves. Just a few were in the water. I recognized Scotty, about eight other waiters and waitresses,

Zola the Canadian pastry girl with the half-inch brow, Mrs. Brady, and a few of the captains. I even saw Mahatma and a couple of his Indian pals sitting up on a grass slope. Everyone certainly looked at me with Della, and I felt proud. I could imagine how happy Mahatma was for me and I didn't want anything to go wrong. A couple of people waved to Della and she waved back. The sound of Bunker's airboat made me speak up.

"You want me to let you off here?" I asked Della.

"No," Della said. "I'll help you paddle back."

There was something about the tone of her voice and the nervous glances she was making that showed she thought it might be a good idea if she did get off at the employees' dock.

"I don't mind," I said.

"Are you sure?"

"Of course I'm sure."

"Well, there's a few things I have to talk over with Zola about the employees' show," Della admitted. "Zola's going to sing backup with a couple of the other girls for my songs."

I didn't mind pulling up and letting everyone get a good look. We weren't more than ten feet away from the dock when Della looked extra nervous, because precisely at that point Bunker came flying into view with a roar. He was alone on the airboat coming around the southern tip of the island at about fifty miles an hour. Della couldn't jump out of the canoe fast enough, but everyone knew Bunker had seen us. There was so much tension in the air you could cut it. "See you later" was all Della said, without looking at me.

"You bet," I said, pushing off and forcing a big smile as though there was nothing unusual going on. I started paddling away from the dock and following the shoreline. Della said one other thing: "Thanks." She called that without looking at me, and just sat quickly next to Zola on a towel and began chatting.

I paddled calmly and began humming "My Baby Takes the Morning Train," and pretended I didn't notice Bunker cutting down the throttle on the airboat. He was practically a thousand feet away, and maybe he had spray on his sunglasses or something and hadn't really noticed anything. Maybe the sun had been in his eyes. I looked back at the dock and saw everyone was still watching me, even Della. When they weren't looking my way, they were glancing out to the airboat. With every stroke I felt safer, and I just wanted to get out of sight of Della, Mahatma, and the employees, but it didn't work out that way. Bunker had let his tremendous airplane engine rest for just a few moments, and then I heard the airboat start to roar again. I pretended it didn't exist, but it certainly did. Bunker got the airboat up to a fantastic speed, so he literally flew over the water off to my left. He raced a good distance to the north and then swung the airboat around in a wide arc, which created a tremendous wake. He completed the half circle just before the employees' dock, and I looked over my shoulder. I saw Mahatma and he looked very worried. Della was standing now calling *"Stop!"* to Bunker, but it was clear to everyone that Bunker was now only interested in me. The airboat closed in on me faster and faster. The waves it caused sprayed out ferociously. He bore down on me. I was helpless. I thought he was going to crash into me. At the last moment he swerved the airboat to the left and created a huge, undulating wall of water. The wave socked into the left side of the canoe, and I was quickly tossed into the lake. I was close enough to shore that I wasn't worried until my head surfaced and I realized I was in water exactly the depth of my body. The canoe was upside down. My left foot had touched bottom. As I tried to push myself upward it slipped between two slimy rocks and my leg was trapped. I could stand, but my mouth could gasp air only during the troughs of the waves. I thought I would drown. I made a quick dive to grab at the rocks. I pulled but nothing gave. I still held my breath and gave another desperate yank. And another. Finally one of the rocks lifted, and my foot scraped out. By the time I surfaced, I had barely enough strength to grab onto the overturned canoe. The only ones who had jumped into the water and were swimming to help me were two of Mahatma's Indians. I was so embarrassed I wished I had died.

Sunday, July 21

1) Ernest Hemingway born, 1899.

2) Turkish proverb: *No matter how far you have gone on a wrong road, turn back.*

3) At the zoo, Della could hardly look at me when she told me she was sorry Bunker had wiped me out. I am disgraced. The only one who talks normally to me is Mahatma, who wants me to come down to Indian House. I can tell he wants to advise me, so I told him no. The whole broiler section laughs at me. Bunker told me it wasn't nice to take other people's girlfriends out in canoes, and called me "Snooks" seven times.

4) I'm thinking of quitting. Mr. Micci stiffed me four dollars again.

Monday, July 22

I believe I have a faulty aorta. Perhaps I've had a stroke. I can't write.

Tuesday, July 23

Still can't write. I pray my father writes me special delivery telling me he's missed me very much and is leaving in his Chrysler New Yorker to see me immediately.

Wednesday, July 24

My diary may really be dead. I didn't go to see Della in the employees' show.

Thursday, July 25

England's first "test-tube baby" born, 1978.

Everyone says Della did a superb job on "My Heart Belongs to Daddy."

I miss Penelope very much.

I tried reading back copies of the *Bayonne News & Sun*. I'm writing the editors that they're using too much hype:

A) STEVEN SPIELBERG, THE POWERHOUSE PRINCE OF HOLLYWOOD, "DRAMATICALLY DREAMS FOR A LIVING"

B) GORBACHEV SENSATIONALLY OUSTS FORMER RAVING RIVAL ROMANOV FROM POLITBURO

C) CHEWING TOBACCO AND SNIFFING SNUFF ARE SWEEPING AMERICAN YOUTH LIKE CABBAGE PATCH DOLLS

D) NEW YORKERS EN MASSE COOKING IN MICROWAVE OVENS. THESE COOL COOKERS ARE SIZZLING HOT!

Friday, July 26

Sent letter to Penelope. Here is text:

Dear Penelope,
Enclosed please find fifty dollars for you to buy Chanel No. 5 or Kangaroos Sneakers. I'm depressed. The

flora and fauna at Lake Henry are impressive. I am having problems socially. Is Mr. Mayo really sleeping in my bed, or did Mom write me that to drive me insane? How can she cherish an ex-hit man? Please burn this letter when you finish reading it. There is something very wrong with my personality. People of all ages hate it. I only want people to like me, but it never works out that way. I go to stores, and if my bill is six dollars and twenty-two cents I give them a ten and twenty-two cents so all they'll have to give me back is four dollars, but they snarl. I wish we could have spoken more before Mom banished me. How can you stand it? Isn't it too early for her menopause? It's been so long since you and I have had a heart-to-heart. I just hope things aren't too terrible for you. Are you all right at the dry goods job? Perhaps I have some kind of sexual dysfunction. I'm making money, so I'll be able to help you with college. I've never been able to do my share, and I'm hoping I don't get fired or hang myself before the summer is over. Don't worry about me. How are you? Have you made any new friends? I think about ghastly things lately. Like the time Mom hired that baby-sitter for us who had a glass eye. I want so much to be rich and famous. It'd be nice if I were even socially bearable. I think of you a lot. I mainly remember the photo of you with long blond hair and me with short curly hair when you were nine and I was six. We were sitting on the hood of Dad's car when he lived with us. Don't be bitter. I'm not. Write to me soon. My only real friend up here is a Hindu. When you came home for the summer I heard you crying in your room. I'm sorry I wasn't adult enough to ask you why. It's easier for me to ask in writing. What's wrong with me? Am I a cripple? Why don't people like me? My phobias have become worse. *I'm apprehensive about getting hit by lightning or contracting encephalitis. Don't worry about me. Are we in transition? Things have to get better. Write me soon. I'm afraid I'm not going to be a genius or intellectual.*

> Your loving brother,
> Eugene

Saturday, July 27

1) Alexandre Dumas (fils) born, 1824.
2) Nudity again dominates the news:
   A) FIREMEN SAVED A CALIFORNIA NUDIST CAMP FROM BURNING AND WERE HONORED WITH A PICNIC LUNCH. OVER 200 FIREMEN AND THEIR FAMILIES SHOWED UP STRIPPED DOWN TO ENJOY THE REPAST SERVED BY THE GRATEFUL SUN WORSHIPERS
   B) NAKED SOVIET WOMEN HAVE TURNED A BLACK SEA BEACH INTO A MECCA FOR BLACK MARKET GOODS. THE KGB IS TOO EMBARRASSED TO RAID
   C) FLYING SAUCER SEEN BY AUSTRALIAN MOTHER SUPERIOR

Sunday, July 28

Johann Sebastian Bach died, 1750.

Micci stiffed another four dollars. His table and the laxative table still staying on. Check-ins added new look alikes. The Four Horsewomen of the Apocalypse now have been replaced by Margaret Thatcher, Mamie Van Doren, Tokyo Rose, and Ray "Boom Boom" Mancini.

Monday, July 29

1) Van Gogh commits suicide, 1890.
2) Went to bank.
3) Got note from Laurette on butterfly-shaped card:

Dear Eugene,

Your father was very happy to hear from you. He wants me to thank you for your generous invitation. We do plan to visit my family in Quebec during August. Perhaps we'll stop by and take you out for lunch on our swing home.

Sincerely,
Laurette

4) I was so happy to hear from Dad's girlfriend I went to the library. They only had *Adieux: A Farewell*

to Sartre by Ms. de Beauvoir. I looked up existential-
ism in the *Encyclopedia Britannica* and found out it was
Sartre's philosophy that one needs to take responsibility
for one's own actions in a godless universe. It was
depressing. The nice librarian was helpful as usual and
told me everything she knew about Simone and Jean-
Paul. They were on-again, off-again lovers for decades
but stayed closest friends and intellectual companions
until Sartre's death. Simone really got around. She
really learned a lot from Jean-Paul but had to run away
and live in the woods. She also made Jean-Paul smarter.
I read the whole book before the evening meal. A lot of
it was boring. The librarian said one book of Simone's
is about a *ménage à trois*. I'll bet they caused havoc at
Notre Dame. Am also still reading *The Last of the
Mohicans*. I'm having trouble figuring out who anybody is.

Tuesday, July 30

1) The Beatles closed their boutique on Baker Street,
London, 1968.

2) Bought antique public-school autograph book at
flea market next to Loudon's Landing Mobil station. It
cost one dollar and has poignant entries dated June 24,
1927 to a girl called Ruth. Sample excerpt:

> *To Ruth—*
> *I wish you health*
> *I wish you wealth*

I wish you gold in store—
I wish you heaven after death
What can I wish you more!
Your sister-grad-U-8,
Louise Kohmick

3) I'm so much in love with Della my heart hurts. The pain is terrible and I don't know what to do.

Wednesday, July 31—Midnight

Decided to watch the employees' show in the club under the dining room. After serving dinner I went back to my room to wash and change. Mrs. Brady told me the guests drink and dance first. Then around 10:30 P.M. the staff performs. Then the guests drink and dance more. About ten I went around the left side of the zoo annex and followed the sound of music. I had no intention of Della seeing me, and I knew only the performing employees were allowed in the dressing-room area. Employees who want to watch have to stand on the lawn outside one of the glass sliding doors.

By the time I got there several waiters, bellhops, and captains were standing around in the shadows while the guests were doing bossa novas and bunny hops. Everybody was having a very good time. I could see the staff cheering section was excitedly waiting. At 10:30 the band gave a drumroll. Alfredo came to the microphone.

"You'll be amazed at their many professional talents," he observed. He concluded his introduction by saying, "And now, ladies and gentlemen, it's show time at the Lake Henry Hotel."

He built the whole thing up like the Ringling Brothers Circus was about to begin. The band started vamping and this one pear-shaped waiter called Huey came out and said he was the master of ceremonies. Then he did a puppet show in which he stood on two chairs and had a little Fred Astaire marionette and a little Ginger Rogers marionette dance and sing "Puttin' on the Ritz." It was very rousing, and even if the marionettes didn't exactly look like they were dancing, the music was scintillating and Huey got a big round of applause. Some of the guests whistled, and a lot of them were loaded and not merely festive and sophisticated like they were during meals. Next, Zola the Canadian pastry chef with the half-inch brow was introduced, and she sang a French song of all things. She said the title translated meant "My World May Be Lonely But I Will Wait for You." She had a very lovely voice, which didn't go with her face at all. As she was singing mellifluously, Scotty came across the lawn and whispered in my ear, "She's a lesbian." I just moved away from him and enjoyed the rest of her touching rendition. Next, Huey introduced a bartender who sang "Ave Maria" and "Let's Get Physical." Then Huey got up on two chairs again and worked a bevy of twelve little Rockette marionettes who kicked their legs in unison to "You're a Grand Old Flag." The audience cheered this number and found it highly patriotic.

Now it was Della's turn.

I gasped when I saw her.

She was wearing a voluminous white fox stole bor rowed from one of the guests. She looked more gor geous than any girl who ever walked the earth. The guests, Alfredo and his staff, and all of us out on the lawn were silent. Della's dark eyebrows and scarlet, perfect lips set against her white skin and the glowing plush fur made her look more arresting than anything ever seen in a Fred the Furrier TV ad. She was flanked by three waitresses as backup on each side, one of whom was Zola. They didn't have fox stoles, so when the spotlight hit them you could see they had made their matching strapless gowns out of red-dyed sheets. The band started playing a pounding beat as Della started to sing delicately and vulnerably:

> *While tearing off a game of golf*
> *I may make a play for the caddie*
> *But if I do, I don't follow through*
> *'Cause my heart belongs to Daddy. . . .*

I mean, that's all the words I can remember. After she sang the song once around she let the stole slip off her shoulders and began to slink with the other waitresses, who now sang with her as they moved. It was breathtaking. My heart filled with sadness knowing she was now so high on a pedestal it was dizzying. I was blinded by the pain. She wound up the song with another, more vigorous chorus and dramatically tossed the fur away at the final moment.

When the enthusiastic applause died down, Della gave the fox fur back to a woman in the audience, went back to the microphone and started singing her second selection:

> *What's the use of wonderin'*
> *If he's good or if he's bad,*
> *Or if you like the way he wears his hat?*
> *Oh . . .*

Della was still accompanied by the girls in red-dyed sheets and now I could notice she was wearing a similar frock made from a red-dyed sheet too. The choreography wasn't as intricate as her "up" number. She and the girls just sort of swayed back and forth. It was very touching, and I was so caught up in her presentation I didn't even notice that Mahatma and a few of the other Indians had accumulated in the shadows to my left. By this point more than forty of the staff had arrived to watch. When Della finished we on the lawn applauded too. Then Huey introduced Captain Pegeen and the salad chef, and they began to execute a tango to the strains of "Orchids in the Moonlight." In the middle of that performance, Della and her backups came out a side door to accept the congratulations of the staff on the lawn. The girls hadn't changed, because they had to wait around for final bows. I impulsively moved toward her, wanting to tell her how impressed I was. The love I felt was now so intense it outweighed my mortification from the canoe incident. I was just about to reach her when a shadow stepped in front of me.

"Where you goin', Snooks?" the shadow asked. I squinted and could see Bunker smiling at me.

"I want to compliment Della," I said.

"I told you not to come near her, Snooks," he said, laughing. Then he suddenly slipped his right foot behind me and shoved his hand into my face. I fell backward so hard on the lawn I rolled ten feet. Bunker strolled toward me. I was afraid he'd kick me, but I was more terrified Della would notice me being worked over again. Then, suddenly—before Bunker could reach me—Mahatma and his crew stepped to block him. It was Buddhakariskaman who helped me up, as Mahatma quietly, firmly told Bunker to get away from me. A lot of the staff were looking now, and before I could stand straight Della saw me as well. She charged directly for Bunker and sized up what had happened in a second.

"I told you to leave him alone!" she yelled at Bunker over the band's second percussion-filled chorus of "Orchids in the Moonlight."

She pushed him aside and came to me. "Did he hurt you?" she asked. "Did he?"

"No," I stuttered, sick to my stomach.

She turned back to Bunker and really started telling him off. He still just had a good laugh and took her by the arm. He led her back to the stage door.

I wanted to die. Just completely die. I hurt so much I couldn't breathe. In a second Huey was out on the lawn screaming for the performers to get back inside and line up for a curtain call. Bunker marched Della back in toward the dressing room area. I was thankful she couldn't see me as Mahatma took my right arm and Buddhakariskaman took my left and they helped me stumble away. I was a loser. As they would say in *The Last of the Mohicans,* I had "shown the white feather." The only grain of spirit which kept my heart beating at all was the knowledge Della had cried out in my defense.

As we passed the zoo, Mahatma signaled Buddhakariskaman to walk ahead with the other Indians. Then we all cut from the zoo path to the end of the front parking oval. There the driveway became Skunks Misery Lane. Mahatma withdrew his arm from supporting me and I walked at his side down the road toward the bridge and Indian House. Headlights from a car suddenly came up the hill and we cut farther onto the shoulder. A stretch Lincoln Continental raced by and I could smell somewhere a skunk had been hit. I was trembling, desperately ashamed, but I remember certain events occurred:

1) We arrived at Indian House. It was dark inside until they got tons of candles burning.

2) Chicken parts started sizzling away in the tandoori oven.

3) Mahatma took me to stand in front of the statue of Shiva. The other brown bodies floated through the flickering light at the opposite end of the room.

4) Mahatma didn't make any conversational demands. He talked to the statue.

5) The smell of curry was strong.

6) Mahatma rubbed Shiva's third eye. He made several circle gestures with his right hand and chanted a prayer about a person called Elias rescuing Nur Ad-Dahr from the sea.

I excused myself to use the bathroom.

7) The bathroom was filled with paintings of leaping fish, twisted tree trunks and a slaughtering with the title *Rao-Bhoj-Singh of Bundi Slays a Tiger*.

8) I went back to Mahatma and he had put on a robe. It had the usual freaky designs, like a mace in the form of a lotus bud and figures lounging on a pavilion.

9) He rubbed Shiva's third eye again. His high squeaky voice delivered an incantation in Hindi.

The next thing I remember Mahatma led me out a back door.

There was an old boathouse with a dock attached. Between the moon and starlight it was easy to make it out to the end and sit down with our feet hanging over the edge. I checked to make certain none of the other Indians had followed us. I could still see the statue of Shiva inside the house through one of the windows. From the dock Shiva was in a glowing profile.

Mahatma and I just sat next to each other in silence.

I calmed down.

It was really a very beautiful spot.

The lake water was dead still, and the island bridge was only a stone's throw away. It was well lighted ever since the social season had begun, and from this vantage point it reflected perfectly in the water.

After a while Mahatma was so silent I felt I was having a session with a strict Freudian analyst.

"What's the answer?" I decided to mutter.

Mahatma laughed.

I was offended.

"Why are you laughing?" I wanted to know.

"You remind me of Gertrude Stein's last words on her deathbed," he said. "Her friends asked her, 'What's the answer?' After two minutes Gertrude just said, 'What's the question?' and died."

I was really impressed Mahatma knew about Gertrude Stein. I thought he'd only know about maybe the history of the Taj Mahal.

"You told me you knew secrets?" I reminded him.

"Yes. And I still know you need them."

"Then tell me *the* secret," I said, my eyes looking straight out at the bridge.

"Which one?"

"The secret of Life." I decided to start at the top.

"That's simple."

"Then what is it?"

"Reversal."

"Reversal?"

"Yes, reversal." He tapped me hard on my shoulder with the knuckles of his right hand. It was a strange way to emphasize a point.

"That doesn't help," I complained, rubbing the spot where his fingers had poked me.

"What help do you need?"

"You told me you knew what I needed."

"If you ask the right question I will tell you the answer."

"Can you tell me the *right* answer?"

"Only *my* answer."

"Would it be strictly a Hindu answer?"

"I told you I'm not orthodox. I borrow answers from Confucius or Emily Dickinson, if need be," he chuckled.

"Why are you willing to share what you know?"

"What I know is like a lamp. A lamp is not good under a table. It must be put on top of the table so all can see."

He went silent again, and I blurted out the main thing on my mind. "How can I make Della love me?"

"Simple," he said. "You have to love yourself first." Then he made one of his weird circle gestures again. "See, that is reversal. The answer is always the opposite of what you think. You don't like yourself, so how will other people like you?"

"I like me," I lied.

"You hate you."

Now I wanted him to shut up, but he didn't. He kept on.

"Della is not able to appreciate you because you don't appreciate you. You are hostile and bitter. You have no light in you about yourself."

"And I suppose you have a light in you?"

"Yes."

"I'd have too if I ate as much curry."

"See? You are hostile." He tapped me hard again on the shoulder and I felt like shoving him off the dock to show him how I wasn't hostile in the least. Then I remembered he was just a nice old man trying to help me as best he could.

He went on. "Lonely people often do not know they ave no self-esteem. You are lonely. That is why you urt. You don't notice how much you put yourself own. You don't come to grips with the fact that your ain comes from your own heart. You are your own orst enemy. You're lonely because you don't know ow to love yourself, and this is what drives other eople away from you like water buffaloes."

"I don't have herds running away from me. I don't now herds," I moaned.

"You need to stop abusing yourself and start treating ourself in a more loving and responsible way."

"Next you're going to tell me I knocked myself own on the lawn before. And I'm the one who swamped e in the canoe. Let me ask you that question. How can stop Bunker from working me over?"

"When you see a loud and vexatious person, you nould keep away. You cross the street."

"But I'm already a coward."

"Crossing the street is not cowardly. It's the same as you see a harlot. You cross the street."

"Are you calling Della a harlot? Della's an angel."

"I never saw an angel sing 'My Heart Belongs to addy.' "

"Oh, you're way off," I told him. "Della is sweet nd gentle. And she's very intellectual and talented."

"She is nice but she has problems. You just lust after er."

I thought I was hearing things. "I *what?*"

"You only lust for her."

"I do not."

"What do you call it then? Love? You love only her ace and body. That's lust."

"I had a whole canoe ride with her."

"And the devil punished you."

"I don't see you with any girlfriends. You or yo[ur] buddies."

"We leave our wives in Detroit. Every summer th[ey] like a nice rest from us, and we like a nice rest fr[om] them."

"You're married?"

"I had a first wife who possessed a philosophy si[m]ilar to mine, and we loved deeply for seventeen yea[rs.] My second wife was a big mistake. She is boisterou[s.] She yells at me and uses four-letter words."

"What do you do?"

"I speak softly and gently close doors. I never sla[m] them. If she is rotten in the shopping mall, I go aw[ay] from her to Burger King."

Now I didn't speak. I decided he read things like t[he] Koran and Dead Sea Scrolls just to learn things to blo[w] people's minds. A few more cars passed by. Two we[re] old ones with dented fenders, which belonged to t[he] staff, and one was a guest's El Dorado.

Mahatma and I sat for about the next ten minutes ju[st] looking at the Milky Way. Then I heard voices. Som[e] employees were dribbling across the bridge heading f[or] town. I recognized a couple of the waiters, the hot[el] hairdresser, a few bellhops, and Captain Pegeen carryi[ng] her pillow. After them came a familiar voice.

It was Louie's, the assistant maître d'. Also, I di[s]tinctly heard Della. A moment later they emerged in[to] the night. They were strolling hand in hand down t[he] lane onto the bridge. It surprised me, Della holdi[ng] hands with Louie. I knew they couldn't see Mahatn[a] and me in the shadows of the boathouse, but the[y] themselves were lit up like on a stage. I couldn't mak[e] out everything they were saying, but Louie was finish[ing]

94

ing eating something from a bag. After a moment he just threw the bag and leftovers over his shoulder, littering the road. When they reached the Loudon's Landing side of the bridge Della stopped and looked at the moon. Louie shockingly took advantage of the moment and put his arms around her. He kissed her like an animal. It looked like he was still chewing, and I could tell from Della's body language she was very uncomfortable. She did reach her right hand up to hold the back of his head, which gave the impression she was enjoying the kiss, but I knew she was only being considerate and didn't want to hurt Louie's feelings. She couldn't have let him kiss her for more than five or six minutes, and then she made him let go of her and they walked on. I really felt sorry for her as Louie again intruded his arm around her shoulder and kissed her neck. They disappeared into the darkness on the Loudon's Landing side. I let them go on their way for a long while before I finally spoke to Mahatma again.

"What if I don't want to cross the street?" I asked him. "What if I don't want to run away from the boisterous ones? What if I want to hold my ground and win?"

"I already told you that secret."

"What?"

"Reversal." He made another circle gesture in the air.

"I don't understand."

"Reversal is something nobody can teach. You are a bright boy. One day when you are ready, you will understand."

Just then I noticed something moving into the lighted part of the island road. At first I thought it was a three-foot mutant black centipede. As it moved farther it appeared much like a huge Angora cat.

"What's that?" I pointed.

"Skunk."

Mahatma was right. I could then see it was the most chimerical skunk I'd ever seen. I guess I'd only really seen skunks in zoo brochures or on the Disney channel. This living skunk was unlike any of those. Its fur was so long it literally touched the ground. It was a majestic creature with its rich, shiny coat broken by two parallel stripes of beautiful white. It moved regally to inspect the food bag Louie had tossed.

I was so zeroed in watching the animal I wasn't aware of the headlights appearing on the lane. It turned out to be two cars speeding from different directions. One car headed down out of the dark island pinewoods that hid the hotel, and the other was coming fast past Buzz-Ro-All.

When I finally realized what was going on, I bolted upright. The skunk was paying no attention to the danger. I started shouting from the dock. The skunk heard me, turned and looked, but still just stayed in the road. I yelled again and again. Mahatma began to clap his hands loudly and bang a piece of wood next to him on the dock. The cars were now bearing down closer and closer and only at the last moment did the skunk turn and glide off into the safe, dark woods.

Thursday, August 1

1) Yves St. Laurent born, 1936.

2) Shredded wheat patented, 1893.

3) Had a dream that I made love to Della. It was an ecstatic experience.

4) Finished *The Last of the Mohicans* by James Fenimore Cooper. Still had awful time figuring out who were the good Indians and who was occupying which forts. In the movie version all the women live and smile a lot and act grateful to the guide, Hawkeye, and the guys who rescue them. In the book the girls get knocked off. The most fascinating aspect of the book was the jacket. The author was born in New Jersey.

5) Della came over to my station during the lunch buffet and told me that she was sorry about what Bunker did to me and that she had told him she was never going out with him again. I told her she was the most amazing girl I'd ever met and that she was exceedingly more talented than Patti LaBelle or Julie Andrews. She looked so grateful for my sincere praise, her eyes lit up. She invited me for an afternoon *café au lait* at her home. She said she'd let me know the best day. She said she'd also bake madeleine cakes. I told Mahatma.

Friday, August 2

1) Fact: There is a live-minnow-eating festival held every year in Geraardsbergen, Belgium.

2) Wild Bill Hickok shot in a saloon in Deadwood, 1876.

3) I can't wait for my visit to Della's. She told me straight off at breakfast it would be next Thursday. I've decided to speed-read everything about the French I can find. I've also decided I'm going to confess my love for her after the *café au lait*.

Saturday, August 3

1) England's Queen Mother and Dolores Del Rio born.

2) "If I'd done everything I'm credited with, I'd be speaking to you from a laboratory jar at Harvard." —Frank Sinatra.

3) Disturbing stories in *Bayonne News & Sun:*
   A) TEENAGE MOM SELLS BABY FOR PAIR OF ROCK CONCERT TICKETS
   B) MAYOR SHOOTS STEPDAUGHTER DURING GUN-SAFETY LESSON
   C) HOROSCOPE WARNS WOMAN: DO NOT TRAVEL BY ROLLER SKATES. SHE DID, SHE DIED!

4) Am beginning to outline what I want to tell Della about my feelings for her.

5) Couldn't sleep. I wonder if Della's mother will be home for our *café au lait*.

6) Have begun reading *The Count of Monte Cristo* and *Cyrano de Bergerac*. They are both about troubled Frenchmen with love problems.

7) Went to Moon Valley butcher and bought Mrs. Brady a $12.49 Genoa salami. She was thrilled.

8) Picked up six orders of broiled kippers from Bunker. He said, "I'm going to kill you, Snooks."

Sunday, August 4

1) Special Delivery initiated, 1889.

2) Micci stiffed again. Am keeping tally.

3) Am really thinking about everything Mahatma told me. I kissed myself in a mirror.

4) In my *History of the World*, today I read about the French Revolution, Robespierre, and Marie Antoinette.

Monday, August 5

1) "Never invest your money in anything that eats or needs repairing."—Billy Rose

2) Went to library. Read in encyclopædia that French women are virtually undisputed in their control of 80

percent of the family budget. Also read about bouilla-baisse, topless sunbathing in San Tropez, and Charle-magne.

3) Made bank deposit.

4) Received letter from Penelope. Here is text:

Dear Eugene:

Got your letter postmarked July 26. Sorry I haven't written sooner. It was very wonderful of you to send fifty dollars. Please don't send any more. I'm making decent money, and as long as I don't get fired I'll have enough for fall semester at New Paltz. Then if I work nights at college I'll be okay for the spring as well. I was sorry to hear you're depressed. It's no picnic down here either, but I'm getting much tougher. Mr. Mayo is sleeping in your bed, and he stinks of cigars. I told Mom I don't think it's right, but she didn't do anything about it. I told her if she loves him so much why not just move him into her room and admit to me they've got a thing going. I know you don't approve of their relationship, but it sure takes a load off of me. That doesn't mean she's not still giving me sex lectures. I've started going out with a very nice boy from the store. His name is Warren. He's tall and gentle and very sweet. Mom hates him because he doesn't make a big fuss over her. The only boyfriend I had she ever ap-proved of was Jimmy the Coast Guard officer. She liked him because he sucked up to her. Remember? Always brought her lilies of the valley, and took her to see A Chorus Line. Well, Warren doesn't suck up to her so she's starting up again with all her neurotic crap. She says Warren's just out for sex, says I can't ride in his car with him. She expects me home every night right after work. She says she knew a baby-faced boy like

Warren when she was growing up and all he had was sex on the brain. She checks my underclothes in the hamper. I told Warren Mom's insane, and he accepts it because his father's insane. You know that book you gave me on Peruvian poetry? Well, I finally got around to reading it. Something made me pick it up the night after I got your letter and the latest "Sex is dirty" lecture. I was very moved by the poem about the brother and sister, where the sister tells the brother she's very ashamed of being born. Remember that one? She's so ashamed she asks her brother if perhaps they should become wolves and he says no. Finally she asks him if they should escape their shame by becoming the sun and the moon and he agrees. Do you remember it? I think you and I have been made to feel very ashamed of ourselves. I know you don't exactly hate Mom or Dad or anyone for making you into what you are. But I do. I hate them both. Maybe "pity them" is more like it. Remember at the end of the poem the brother and sister grab torches and run around outside their mud huts as fast as they can until they become glowing balls and fly up into the sky? The sister then decides she wants to be the sun and so she blows the brother's glow out, and he becomes the cold moon. That's where you and I differ from the poem, Eugene. I am already the moon. I am the moon and I hate Mom and Dad for chilling me. You still have fire in you. You mustn't let anyone put it out. If you want to be a famous writer you will be that. I have too much anger for anything so noble. I'm out for me from here on in. I have a sicko for a mother and a bastard for a father but they're not going to knock me out of orbit. I've got crater marks all over me. I'm going to end up with a middle-class career, a husband and children and live as far away from Bayonne as I

*can get. I'll always attract only weak men. I'm far more
calculating than even you can know. I'll get what I want
because I'm not asking for very much. I'll have the
mediocre, not you. You have a dimension of forgiveness
I'll never know. In a funny way one day you may have
to thank me for only one thing: I was born three years
before you, so I took most of the crap. They took their
best shots at me. You almost escaped, but not quite. If
you ever need me just let me know. I'll fight any battle
you need. If anybody tries to hurt you, I'll smash them
without guilt, without conscience and without regret.
I'll kick ass. You're going to make it, Eugene. Believe
it. You'll be the sun for both of us.*

> *Your loving sister,*
> *Penelope*

I realized that I had two people who really believed in
me now. Penelope *and* Mahatma. I hope they can meet
each other one day.

Tuesday, August 6

1) "Writing is like giving birth to a grand piano."
—Stephen Vincent Benét

2) Read about Joan of Arc's life and death. She was a
very special person. I wish I could have gotten to know
her.

3) Picked up three orders of broiled haddock, and
Bunker said, "Snooks, I'm going to tear your face
off." He must have found out I'm going for *café au lait*.

4) I'm going to ask Della to marry me.

Wednesday, August 7

1) First rugby game played to Australian rules.
2) Mata Hari born, 1876.
3) Della told me she's already baked the madeleines.
4) Librarian brought in her own book on the Louvre museum. Excellent photos of Mona Lisa and a mummy. Librarian said Paris has superb croissants.
5) I'm so happy I decided to forgive my best friend, Calvin Kennedy, and wrote to him inquiring how he was and asking him to bring me up to date on all the gang in Bayonne. I was honest and told him he hadn't heard from me because I had felt hurt he had told me he was vomiting in bed with 104° fever and then I saw him screaming "great melons" at a girl from Jake Cahill's car. I had to be honest and begged him to be honest with me.
6) I now definitely think it will be appropriate to discuss with Della our marital future.

Thursday, August 8

1) Seven hundred New York teachers protest they could not teach if allowed to whip pupils with only a strap instead of a rod, 1827.
2) a) VOODOO CURSE CHANGES WOMAN INTO TREE

3) Finished learning key French expressions such as *affaire d'amour, savoir-faire* and *bouillon*.

4) By 2:30 I was in the Loudon's Landing Flower Boutique purchasing an FTD-type arrangement of white roses entwined with ferns and baby's breath. I also bought a two-pound box of Whitman's chocolates, special nut selection, at Sav-On Drugs.

Della gave me her address, and I had no trouble finding it because I'd once seen her head up that way.

I was very nervous walking past the row of wobbly woodframe houses with sagging porches, but certainly not as nervous as if Bunker had happened to drive by. Up close the houses looked like they had been crushed by avalanches. Della's wasn't the one with the turret, or bell tower. Even in the daylight that one looked like a spa for fox bats. Her exact address was 163 Hear Ye Road, and the name on the mailbox was Mitford. Della Mitford. I had never even asked her last name. I did figure it wasn't going to be Santini or Pasquale, because it was only her mother who was from Sicily. Della had told me her father was English, so Mitford sounded right, but to me Della should have had a last name like *de la Tour*. Della de la Tour. She could use that as a stage name or nom de plume and be very successful, I feel.

Now I might as well get it right. The house looked like a disaster area from the outside. It was a long, two-story rectangle of decaying wood, dull stucco, and rusty shingles with a cracking cement foundation and chipped steps on its right front corner. It was set back about two hundred feet from the road and sitting on at least two acres of land. My other observations were:

1) There were what looked like petite pens and chicken shacks in the backyard.

2) I heard a gaggle of geese honking like maniacs.

3) A long grape arbor covered the front walk with lush leaves and bunches of green grapes hanging all over.

4) Slate pieces of the walk were crooked.

5) It was picturesque.

I was excited and frightened, mixing up all the romantic things I wanted to tell her, as I walked up and rang the buzzer.

After a few moments Della answered, attired as the most beautiful French country girl in the world. She had on an earth-colored, low-cut dress with a little white apron, and she brushed her casually glamorous hair away from her face as though she'd just come from slaving over a hearth.

"*Bonjour,*" she said.

"*Bonjour,*" I replied.

She let me in and I presented her with the flowers.

"Oh, they're beautiful," she said.

"Thanks," I said.

"Is your mother home?" I asked.

"Yes." She rolled her eyes as though we were speaking of an ogress.

"I brought candy for her."

"You shouldn't have," she said with a special edge.

She led me down a hallway. I caught a glimpse of a stairway going up on my right, and a sliding door to my left that wasn't completely closed, so I could see the living room at the front of the house looked like an Adirondack annex for the Collier brothers. My pulse rate was now over 170 beats a minute. We went into a middle room, which looked like it should have been a dining room because it had a brass and glass chandelier, but it was clearly used as a bedroom with a sewing machine. Clothes were thrown all over everything. The stuff wasn't hanging on the walls like an explosion had taken place. Everything just looked like someone very neatly had put one thing on top of the other, coats, dresses, newspapers, boxes, and books for years and years. I would say incessant stacking seemed to have taken place. Even a grand piano in one corner was covered with sheet music, towels, photographs, and the one main shot Della had told me about—an 8 × 10 of her father in uniform stood looking at me from a frame made of large bullet shells. He looked like a very nice, innocent man with brown hair and a trim moustache. A hard-working, semi-corpulent woman sat at the black-with-yellow-pinstripes sewing machine making it whirl away.

"Mother," Della said, tapping the woman on the shoulder.

"What?" Her mother jumped, stopping the machine.

"Mother, this is Eugene."

The woman turned to look at me, focusing over a pair of wire-frame glasses.

"I'm very pleased to meet you, Mrs. Mitford," I said.

Della's mother stood up. A big, warm smile broke across her face. She looked extremely intelligent in a bucolic sort of way. Her dress looked like she had gone to Capri for a weekend and bought it at a better fire sale.

"Just some candy," I mumbled, placing the box in her hands.

Now she absolutely glowed, and I could see straight off she liked me.

"Oh, my, thank you," she said. "It's very nice of you."

"It's nothing."

"It's good to finally meet you, Eugene. Della's told me so much about you."

"She has?"

That really made me feel good.

"Yes. I'm so glad she invited you over. Come"—she winked—"let's go out to the kitchen." She was as spry as anything as she led the way, but I could feel tension between her and Della. I couldn't exactly figure out why. I thought her mother looked and sounded very good-natured. She didn't look extraordinarily Sicilian except for her dark hair. Her complexion was regular and she had mature, lovely features. Della certainly inherited a lot of them, although her perfect ears and cheekbones seem to resemble her father's in the photo.

The kitchen was fairly large and was full of good smells. There were pots and pans all over the place with succulent things stewing in them.

"Sit down, Eugene," Mrs. Mitford insisted. "Are you hungry? Would you like some homemade rigatoni?"

Della looked horrified. "Mother, we're having *café au lait* and madeleines."

"That'll be fine for dessert," Mrs. Mitford corrected, "but a growing boy needs a good lunch."

"We already ate at the zoo," Della complained.

"I really couldn't eat anything," I told Mrs. Mitford, but she didn't listen. She put the candy box down and in a flash scooped out twisted noodles from a pot of boiling water, drained them onto a plate and smothered them with luscious tomato sauce.

"Mother, you know madeleines have a delicate flavor. You're going to ruin his taste buds."

"I'm not going to ruin any buds, am I?" she queried me.

"No," I smiled, caught in the middle.

"There, Della—I told you," she bubbled, and flashed me another big grin. She put the plate in front of me and started grating fresh cheese like dandruff. Della caught my eye and rolled her eyes to heaven again. It was quite clear she couldn't stand her mother barging in on her planned menu. It didn't bother me. I just didn't like Della getting upset, because it was clear she had the madeleines and *café au lait* ready to go. In truth, I thought Mrs. Mitford was one of the most considerate and diplomatic mothers I'd ever met. It was only that she wanted to know a little about me. In less than five minutes she had discreetly established my education, my parents' vocations, my religion, career aspirations, hobbies, favorite cuisines, political leanings, sports interests, health plans, inferred love life, favorite school subjects, and mental health. She seemed very pleased. And she didn't just dominate the conversation. I felt Mrs. Mitford had every right to know a few things about me. She had done it without being nosy or obvious, and I was particularly happy because I could tell I had passed inspection with flying colors. She simply spoke her mind with admirable intelligence, grace, and loving concern for her daughter. She was also very giving in return, and let me know that since her husband's death, when Della was two, she'd worked as a telephone operator in Glens Falls, a local seamstress, and a textile mill forelady in Cooperstown. Also she informed me she was Catholic, had twice been in Georgia, three times to Vatican Square to touch the Pope and once on a glider ride in Mohawk Valley. I really found her delightful, and we laughed a lot.

I noticed Della was getting increasingly disturbed, and finally just asked her mother if it wasn't time for her to return to her sewing machine. The stress on Della's part almost polarized the occasion into a struggle over the supremacy of madeleines to rigatoni. Underneath any of Della's interjections I found the distinct sense she wanted to put her mother down for anything Italian while underlining the greater sophistication of anything French. Truthfully, I thought Della was being a bit overly defensive.

Mrs. Mitford excused herself at what I thought was exactly the right moment to let Della and me be alone. She went to the room with her machine, and considerately closed the door. I knew the time would soon be proper for my confessions to Della. I just had to be sensitive and pick exactly the right moment. With Mrs. Mitford closed back up in the sewing area, Della made several cracks about her as she served the dessert. I told her how much I liked her mother and that she should be very proud of her. I could see Della wasn't the least bit interested in hearing anything maternally positive, so I dropped the subject and we had the most glorious *tête-à-tête* about the *Comédie Française* I've ever had in my life.

As I sipped my coffee I decided Mahatma was wrong about my only lusting after Della. There was nothing wrong with a physical dimension to loving someone, and I don't think anyone can put a time clock on anything like that. As little time as Della and I had had to know each other I was certain I deeply loved her. Of course, I had dreamed about how the afternoon might go if Della's mother hadn't been home. I had never considered a complete sensual union over afternoon *café au lait* and madeleines. I had dreamed the most I could possibly accomplish was to make my major confessions and maybe hold her hand and touch her shoulder. I didn't expect to even brush her waist or any more intimate part of her without building up to it over a period of at least six or seven dates. I did, however, dare to dream I would kiss her this afternoon.

Even with the sound of the sewing machine running in the other room, and Della and I gently munching madeleines, I couldn't take my eyes off her lips. I'd come a long way from when I'd first seen her and my emotions had made her lips blur into only generalized facial organs. Now I could see exactly how full they were, how little lipstick she used, and how moist and beckoningly innocent her mouth was. I wished I had enough courage to just place my lips on hers. If only Bayonne High had given a course in Advanced Incipient Kissing, I think a lot of kids would have signed up for it. I thought about *asking* her if I could kiss her, but I decided that was a weak approach. How could she say "yes" without it then being *she* who had been forced to utter the commitment? It was up to me to make the move. Mahatma's words, "You're a watcher, not a doer," went through my head.

What Della and I finally did during the repast, Dear Diary, was as follows:

1) Della brought in her cassette player and played the Paris Philharmonic's version of *Les Sylphides* and *Le Sacre du Printemps,* which she said meant "The Nymphs" and "The Rite of Spring." The percussion seemed filled with hormones.

2) She asked if I'd like some sliced tomatoes with herbs from Provence and I said yes.

3) She told me she was now reading a biography of Colette and that Colette had great panache.

4) She played a record of Edith Piaf singing the French national anthem.

5) She got out a guitar and accompanied herself to "La Vie en Rose."

6) Then, as a naughty non-French departure, she got me to sing along with her in a humorous Marlene Dietrich piece called "See What the Boys in the Back Room Will Have." She did this number especially loud, so her mother would definitely hear.

7) She made a second Teflon tray of hot madeleines.

5) She showed me pictures of her aunt Claire with her ex-mountain lion and also with her dictionary-writing husband walking around the Left Bank of Paris, and a postcard from a famous restaurant called La Tour d'Argent where she and her husband had Duck No. 3,473,221. I was very impressed.

9) She also told me once her aunt Claire was visiting a wild-animal importer in Albany and a gorilla got out of its cage and Aunt Claire almost had to jump out a fourth-story window.

10) She took me into the bedroom, cleared off the piano and ignored her sewing mother while she played "Clair de Lune."

Then her mother told Della she had to feed the geese. My whole body began to shake because I knew now would come the time for me to bare my heart.

Della took me back into the kitchen, slamming the door to the sewing room. Once she was away from her Italian mother she became her usual sweet and Francophilic self again.

"Want to help me feed the geese?" she asked.

"Yes," I said. I could tell she saw a different look in my eyes, but she didn't say anything.

Della perambulated around the kitchen pulling out

half loaves of old bread from various cabinets and tossed them into a handsome wicker basket along with a good dose of goose feed. Then she led me into a small back pantry area and out a rickety back door.

The moment we set foot in the backyard about a hundred geese went bananas. There was a low chicken-wire fence barely keeping them in the huge rear yard. She opened a makeshift gate, and as we stepped into the geese's territory they waddled like mad to surround us.

Della invited me to reach into the basket and break up some of the bread to feed the mob of fat, feathered bodies that pressed in on us. Every second or so one of the geese would try to eat my shoes, pants or hands. I finally realized I could survive even the most rabid of the goose bites with very little pain.

Della really had a good laugh watching me. She looked like a goose's answer to Little Bo Peep, and the birds really adored her.

After three or four turns Della emptied the remainder of the bread and feed in one spot and took the basket with her as she led me away from the distracted whirl-pool of birds and into the main goose barn. She closed the door behind us, and there in the afternoon shadows I saw row upon row of goose nests, many of which had huge eggs in them.

As Della slowly and delicately began to place eggs in her basket, I knew the time had come.

"I'm in love with you, Della," I said softly.

Della paused for a second as though checking out her hearing. Then she continued gathering the big eggs in very slow motion and I was terrified I would have to repeat my words.

"You don't love me, Eugene," she finally said gently.

I was relieved at least I had made a start and she hadn't turned and fled the goose barn.

"I want to marry you. I want to spend the rest of my life with you."

Della still didn't look at me. She stopped moving about but carefully examined the bottom of one egg to clean it of several strands of straw.

"You're a very sweet boy, Eugene."

She sounded very emotional.

"I have tremendous feelings for you, Della. Tremendous."

"You don't know me that well."

"I just have to tell you what is going on inside of me, or I'll die," I said.

Della smiled, her face flushed and brimming with an unmistakable compassion.

"I don't want you to die," she said quietly.

"I have wild, libidinous dreams about you," I blurted. I just had to get everything out the best I could.

"Eugene, I've just met you. We've hardly talked."

She looked at me and appeared sincerely surprised and confused. I guess I hadn't been prepared for this reaction.

"Can I just try to explain?"

"I just don't want you to be hurt," she said, turning her eyes back to egg examination.

"If I can be truthful I won't be hurt," I insisted. "The worst pain I've had all my life is that I've never really shared my feelings with anyone. The best friend in my life is a diary. Isn't that stupid?"

"No, I don't think it's stupid. I think we're both at ages when we don't have that many people to talk to."

"You have no one to talk to either?" I asked, amazed.

"Eugene, I do talk to *some* people," she said. "I've also got to be at least a year older than you."

"You're right. But do you think that'll make any difference when you're eighty-four and I'm eighty-three?"

"It doesn't make much difference now. I'm just saying maybe I do have some friends I open up to. A lot of kids I know don't. It must be a very frightening thing, and a year at our age usually makes a big difference, at least to ourselves."

"I know you talk to Bunker."

"Yes, I do."

"But you told me you weren't his steady girlfriend. And I saw you with Louie . . ."

"Where?" she wanted to know.

"Around," I said. I really hadn't quite gotten over the vision of her and Louie on the bridge.

"Louie and I have been friends since the third grade. He used to get left back all the time just so we'd be together. He's really very nice. He has no *savoir-faire*, but he's been a good Adirondack friend. . . ."

She looked absolutely sincere, and I know she was being dead honest. I was sorry I had even brought up Louie's name.

"I can only open up when I write," I said.

"Many writers are like that, don't you think?" She had such profound understanding of a belles-lettres personality.

"But I don't want only that," I protested. "I want to live in the real world. I can't take the chance of letting this whole summer pass by without your knowing how possessed I am by you."

She silently collected two more eggs, and then answered very considerately.

"If talking it out will make you feel better, I don't

mind. If it's going to make you feel worse, then don't. I don't know what else to say.''

''Whenever I see you my eyes haze over and the blood in my hands, arms and fingers sort of dances.''

''I see,'' she said.

''I had memorized a list of everything I wanted to tell you, but it's not coming out in the right order. God, those are big eggs,'' I said, panicking.

''Did you ever eat a goose egg?''

''No. They must take a long time to soft boil.''

''They're very popular in France.''

''Della, I don't want to talk about oversized eggs. I need to talk about you and me.''

I could see she was disturbed at my change back to emotional stress. ''I've planned to tell you all about our future physical closeness as well. I've got to discuss that, because even if you said you had loving feelings for me, I'd be frustrated if I didn't try to discuss a schedule of intimacy with you,'' I explained.

''Do you mind if I sit down?''

''No, please do. This won't take long. I don't want you to think I've only got sex on my mind. I love your character traits best,'' I stressed.

Della put her basket of eggs down, and we sat on a bale of hay near one of the goose-barn windows.

''Eugene, how can you know anything about my character traits?''

''I know in my heart you have all the important virtues that a girl mate should have. When I look at you I know I can trust you. I always sensed we could communicate. We have many similar interests. We could spend a lifetime talking about Monet's waterlilies, rich sauces, and *The Hunchback of Notre Dame*. I know we'll both probably want to finish high school before we get married, but I've already worked out the geography and present bus and train fares between here and Bayonne. We could visit each other on various weekends. I can double up on courses, catch up to you, and then after graduation we can both study at the Sorbonne in Paris. I never asked you your I.Q. Mine is 139, the highest in the eighth grade at Bayonne's I.S. No. 3, which is the last time I was tested. I know we both have intensive potential to become intellectuals, and you already are a considerable French one. We both have a sense of humor. I laugh at many things and often guffaw. In less than two years we could be nuptialed and eating goat cheese and bread on the banks of the Seine or having ham-and-onion quiches on the Champs-Élysées. I'm not as handsome a boy as you are beautiful a girl, but I am very hardworking, sincere and ambitious. I think we could be inspirations for each other. I think it only fair to tell you now my favorite writers are Shakespeare, Shaw and Ibsen, but I swear I will become very French oriented. Another good quality I think I have is that I am very individualistic. Maybe you've noticed that. After our university graduations I won't be jealous if you're a cultural attaché for the Biarritz embassy or have to balloon weekends to places like Marseilles or the Loire Valley. I would understand and not make you feel guilty. I could teach English as a second language in Limoges if you wanted. I think we're both very natural persons. We wouldn't have any insane ambitions to impress people, which is not to say we wouldn't be *la crème de la crème* of society if you wanted to be."

I was aware of the fact I was rambling out of control and Della was looking at the floor, but I just couldn't stop. "I know we could create a Friday-night salon that would attract the finest artists, writers and philosophers of Pigalle. Our marriage would be so fine. And I think it's only fair that I give you one more specific about our future boudoir life."

"Eugene, there's really no need to . . ."

"I'm a virgin," I told her.

Then, as Chekov would say, "the bird of silence flew over."

Della just sat, still staring at the floor.

I really felt much better now that I had most of the important points out in the open.

"Well," I finally added much more calmly, "I think I've covered everything I should. The general drift is that I think you're irresistibly efflorescent."

Now Della seemed sad more than anything.

"Is something wrong?" I asked.

"No," she said.

We were alone. Just Della, me and the eggs.

We were silent again.

I moved an inch closer.

I put my arm around her.

I kissed her.

I couldn't believe it was happening.

I thought of so many things at the same time ordinary language couldn't capture them. I would have needed a court stenographer.

Some of the things I thought with my lips on hers were:

1) Her breath is like lilacs.

2) Control my tongue.

3) I can't believe she might actually have feelings for me.

4) Her lips are like warm apple slices.

5) I want to move my hand up to her hair.

6) When should I stop?

7) I want her to be the mother of my children.

8) I'm so happy I could die.

At that moment the sound of flapping and squawking geese storming the goose barn reached my ears. I knew the kiss must end, and I glided my lips away from hers. I came back to reality slowly, like waking from an overdose of dental gas.

"Della! Della!" came Mrs. Mitford's voice suddenly, calling over the cacophony of geese.

"Coming, Mother," Della called back.

We stood up. She picked up the basket of goose eggs and started to lead me out.

She gave me a final private look and I could almost swear she was about to weep.

Friday, August 9

1) John Dryden born, 1631.

2) **plau·dit** (plô′dit) *n*. An act of applauding, esp. clapping with hands.

3) Richard M. Nixon resigns with speech about his mother and America's pressing need to produce more plumbers, 1974. His last words were *au revoir*.

4) Della acted strange at the evening meal. I asked her if anything was wrong and she said no, she was just feeling a little under the weather.

Saturday, August 10

Asked Della if she wanted to go for a canoe ride. She said she couldn't because her aunt Claire was coming for a visit and she'd be busy.

Sunday, August 11

Asked Della if she wanted to go to Hairy Mary's for a pizza tonight. She said no, her aunt Claire had arrived and was teaching her French possessive pronouns.

Monday, August 12

Went to bank.
   Received back copies of the *Bayonne News & Sun:*
   A) COED TERRIFIED AS OUIJA BOARD SUMMONS SATAN
   B) COUPLE LIVES IN CENTRAL PARK CAVE
   C) HOW LIZ LOST 43 POUNDS
   Got letter from Mom. Text as follows:

Dear Eugene:

It's taken me a long time to reply to your last letter, because I found it highly offensive. Mr. Mayo has no disease which is going to go into your mattress. If you deliberately were trying to frighten me about not sitting in lighted windows, you succeeded. I even ride hunched down in the Packard. Charlie is not Mafioso. I was only sharing a confidence with you, but I see you're still being very oedipal. I'm also upset about your sending me Madame Bovary. *You must think I'm really stupid. You've had me in a long funk, but I've got everything into perspective now. How are the mountains? I'll bet you're having the time of your life. You really ought to send Aunt Ruth a thank-you note. I haven't lost any more weight, because of cauliflower. I thought I was being so good, eating mainly Wasas, vegetables and Lean Cuisine's oriental beef. Nobody told me when you cook cauliflower it turns into horrible sugar! I am now reading Gail Sheehy's* Pathfinders. *That woman is truly helping me overcome my mid-life crisis. What you don't seem to understand, young man, is that I have a great deal of worth. I have sent appreciation notes to* Psychology Today, Cosmopolitan *and* Playgirl. *You know how when you were eleven you started criticizing me, saying I had a phony laugh? I'd hang up from a phone call and you'd tell me I laughed phony twenty-three times in one phone call? Well, you've got a lot to learn. Laughter doesn't always have to be humorous. Sometimes it's just being polite, or a way of saying "Hello in there" to someone. It's wanting to love and be loved. Penelope is driving me insane. She's dating a filthy-minded, sneaky-looking guy from the dry goods stock department. I don't know how she finds them. I bought her a copy of* Pathfinders *too, but she told me to stuff it.*

She has so much anger in her. She'll probably let herself get knocked up now that her I.U.D. has been declared carcinogenic. I asked her what she was going to use now, and she told me it was none of my business. Lord only knows what she does away at Teachers' College. Am sending six Snickers under separate cover. So long for now.

I really do love you, Eugene, no matter what you think. "Buona fortuna" from Charlie.

Mom

P.S. Charlie took me to Mama Leone's to try fried squid. It's not for everyone. Calvin Kennedy called to say he was going to write to you. I think he was stoned.

Tuesday, August 13

Ian Fleming died, 1964.

Asked Della out. She said she couldn't because her aunt Claire wanted her to go antiquing.

Wednesday, August 14

Duncan slain by Macbeth, 1040.

Asked Della if she'd like to go out after her show tonight. She said she had to go home to help her mother and Aunt Claire pound veal.

Thursday, August 15

Macbeth slain by Malcolm, 1057.

I didn't ask Della out. I can tell she doesn't want to talk to me. She said Aunt Claire was staying at least two more weeks.

Friday, August 16

I am very depressed. I know Della is completely horrified by my confession in the goose barn. Mahatma is constantly trying to draw me out. I don't know how he can care about me.

The Snickers arrived.

Saturday, August 17

Mae West born, 1893.

Asked Della if I had offended her. She said no, it's just that Aunt Claire needs her to visit cousins and other relatives.

Sunday, August 18

I asked *myself* if I wanted to go for a canoe ride and I unfortunately said yes. I had only intended it as part of Mahatma's "Learn to love yourself" advice. I should have known better than to go out on the lake again, because Bunker called me "Snooks" all week, and all I could think of was how could Della ever go out with him. On two occasions he almost drove me to retaliate and ask him if his steroid shots had damaged his frontal lobes. I was also going to tell him he should hurry back to his father's monkey farm because he must be one of the main attractions, but I didn't want to betray Della's confidences to me.

At two o'clock I rented a canoe from Buzz-Ro-All. I thought about buying a rod and reel and taking up fishing but decided there were too many details, such as sinkers, lures, what pound-test line, top or bottom fishing, license, casting, trolling, bass or trout, rowboat vs. canoe, live bait, stringing fish, disengaging swallowed hooks, and filleting. I decided an unembroidered, peaceful canoe ride was more in order.

I won't say I didn't remember what happened last time, but I couldn't let any fears I had about Bunker keep me off the lake for the rest of the summer.

Maybe that was unsound reasoning on my part.

Mahatma said if I ever found a boisterous person in my path I should just cross the street, but he hadn't gone into a great deal of illumination about what to do when on a lake.

On some level I knew the moment I got into the canoe and started paddling that there was a suicidal element to it. I wasn't more than a few hundred feet from the dock when I couldn't help but remember *Crime and Punishment* and the compulsion of a criminal to return to the scene of the crime.

I decided not to look for trouble and to go due north under the bridge and stay close to the hotel island. That took me past the back of Indian House and the boat-house. The rest had only woods along the shoreline, a few trees knocked over by lightning, and a very decrepit gazebo at the northernmost tip. At one time the gazebo had been the end of a strolling path for guests, but that was very long ago.

I paddled past the end of the island. There was a buoy marker for shallow water. Large rocks lay only a few feet under my canoe. At one point it became so shallow my paddle struck bottom. Farther, the floor of the lake dropped off and the water became stark blue again. The breeze rushed at my face, and I began to forget my puzzlement over Della's coldness. I wasn't jealous that she was spending so much time with her aunt Claire. I think every young person needs a worldly and sophisticated adult model to learn from. I hoped she'd want me to meet her aunt. I'd never even heard of any woman who once had any kind of lion for a pet and was nearly crushed to death by a primate in Albany. I considered perhaps my next move should be to invite Della, her aunt Claire and Mrs. Mitford out for mozzarella marinara or eggplant parmigiana somewhere. I felt very insecure.

Far ahead of me was Blue Mountain Bay, but I didn't want to go there. Besides, the wind shifted, which made it difficult for me to proceed.

Freud would say I planned everything that happened then subconsciously, but it seemed sensible to bear right and head back on the other side of the island.

The wind was so strong I had a full workout by the time I headed up the channel to the hotel. Soon the closest landing point was the employees' dock. The rotting wooden platform was really bobbing. Today more than thirty of the staff were sunbathing and rubbing Bain de Soleil on each other. Nobody was swimming. Scotty was there. Alfredo and Louie were sitting on lounge chairs up on the grassy slope. Zola, Mrs. Brady, Captain Pegeen, three broiler chefs, the busboys, and half the zoo staff had their bodies draped in various positions soaking up the rays. The beautician was using a sun reflector. Of course, they all looked at me. I gave them a wave and called out, "Hey, anyone want a ride?" Nobody waved back and nobody answered. Somebody could have at least said, "No, thank you, Eugene." They stared, however. I started paddling past the dock. I found myself starting to sing "Tie a Yellow Ribbon." Then I heard Bunker's airboat.

What happened was a replay.

Bunker roared around the second island at full throttle. This time he had another broiler assistant in the seat next to him. What happened was methodical. Bunker kept his airboat up at high speed. I wouldn't dignify his behavior by paddling scared or rushing for shore. In seconds he was behind my canoe, precisely like the first time. The wake from his boat sprayed high and far. He bore down on me. I thought he was going to run right up my back, but he swerved in time and sent the wall of water at me again. The wave socked into the left side and once more I was flipped into the lake for all to see.

This time I just floated to the top, righted
myself with everyone laughing at me. I sincerely w...
Bunker would be fried in an electric chair or at minimum
sentenced to death by lethal injection.

Monday, August 19

Went to bank. My balance is now six hundred twenty-
three dollars and seven cents.

Called Dad in NoHo. Spoke to Laurette's answering
service. Knew they were already in Quebec. Got address.

Wrote letter to Dad. Here is text:

Dear Dad:

*Am so excited you and Laurette are visiting her fam-
ily in Quebec. Please thank her for letting me know you
might stop by Lake Henry on your way home. Do you
have any idea what day? I work from 7 A.M. to 10:30
A.M., and from 12 noon to 1:30 P.M., and from 6 P.M. to
9:30 P.M. I need to talk to you very badly. I need your
advice. I'm very confused about some things. Please
come. Let me know what day. I'll pay for lobster meals
with drawn butter and the cozy Pine Knoll Motel. It has
a heated pool and slide. I wait desperately to hear from
you. Please, please, please come.*

> *Your loving son,*
> *Eugene*

Tuesday, August 20

Constitution Day, Hungary.

Johnny Weissmuller married Beryl Scott, 1939.

"With a book tucked in one hand, and a computer shoved under my elbow, I will march, not sidle, shudder or quake, into the twenty-first century."—Ray Bradbury.

Asked Della out. She said she had to cook an oregano goose with Aunt Claire.

I asked Scotty out. He said yes. He wants me to buy him Heineken beer at the Airport Inn tomorrow night.

Wednesday, August 21—Midnight

Scotty borrowed the salad chef's 1973 Pinto. We drove fourteen miles to the town of Lake Henry. I was thankful to be far away from the hotel so I wouldn't be tempted to make a fool of myself watching Della in the staff show.

The Airport Inn isn't near any airport.

It's the best dining, dancing and western-music bar within fifty miles, Scotty said. I believe him.

It has a real Piper Cub hanging from the ceiling, and even the bar was six deep. Nobody checks I.D.'s.

Scotty drank seven Heinekens and one Budweiser. I had nine diet colas. A swinging college crowd was all over the place, two-stepping to updated versions of "It Wasn't God Who Made Honky-Tonk Angels" and "Gigi." The noise was deafening. I let Scotty get feeling pretty good before I started pumping him about Della. He said he thought she was stuck-up. Also said last summer she went out with everyone on the staff two times. The ones she went out most with were Bunker, Louie, and Alfredo, the maître d'. I was shocked. I knew about Bunker and Louie but not Alfredo. Scotty said Alfredo took out all the waitresses, because they liked his *Miami Vice* look and Cuban charm. He also said it was very well known among the staff last summer that Della was considered frigid except with Bunker, Louie, and Alfredo. I asked him if she was still going out with Alfredo and he said not much, because Alfredo was busy with eight others including the Loudon's Landing postmistress.

After Scotty had two more beers I asked who he heard Della was going out with this summer. He said besides the aforementioned, she was also dating a lumberjack, an egomaniacal abstract painter with a beard who had built his own H-bomb shelter in the side of a mountain, and some muscle-ridden local yokel who made seashell jewelry.

"She goes out every night of the week," he said.

Right then and there I was sorry I had even wasted any money on buying Scotty Heinekens. He was really a guzzler, and I spent the rest of the night looking up at the Piper Cub on the ceiling while he played an ashtray with swizzle sticks.

The ride back to the dormitory was horrifying. I was already sick to my stomach from the slanderous lies he told about Della.

Thursday, August 22

First dwarf exhibited in America, 1771.

Asked Della to go out tonight. She said she couldn't because her aunt Claire was taking photos of her to submit to the most respected Albany modeling agency.

Went to town. Read *Bayonne News & Sun* at diner, eating homemade blueberry pie à la mode. Provocative articles on HOW MUCH LOVING DO YOU REALLY NEED?, WEDDING BELLS FOR SEX THIMBLE DUDLEY MOORE and ONE-ARMED TEENAGER PLAYS VIOLIN.

I ran into Mrs. Mitford. I wished I was dead.

I deliberately hung around town thinking I'd run into Della and Aunt Claire. I had been to the post office and taken a good look at the postmistress. Then I had the pie and checked the program at the movie theater. The new feature is *A View to a Kill*. I strolled down to the public beach and went into the library and browsed. I went to Main Street and into the underprivileged mall's grocery store. I had a distinct urge for a box of Cheese Niblets and a bag of Reese's Pieces. I was watching live trout in a tank when Mrs. Mitford appeared in the bread section. She was feeling every loaf of Wonder Bread and zeroing in on some Stella D'oro cookies. I wanted to speak, but I couldn't get my mouth moving. She moved away from the bread section, which I thought made sense since I know how much of her own cooking she did.

She checked out the whole-grain selections on top of

the Campbell's soups. She sniffed at several packages of flour and read the entire contents list on a tomato paste can.

"Hello, Mrs. Mitford," I said.

She looked at me as though I was some awful preservative, but then her mature, lovely features softened, and she flashed me a big smile like she had done at the sewing machine.

"Eugene," she said. "What are you doing here?"

"Felt like some Cheese Niblets," I admitted.

"Be careful. So many things are filled with poisons."

She didn't say that with great alarm. She sounded intelligent in her simple manner. The dress she had on looked much better than the Capri flea-market job she had on when she served me rigatoni. She even had put on makeup.

"Actually, I'm very glad to see you," she said.

"You are?" I was shocked.

"I know Della thinks I'm just an old nag, so don't even say I spoke to you, all right?" She winked.

"Is something wrong?"

"I can't tell you how happy I am that you've been going out with Della."

"You can't?"

"I really am glad she has such a good friend in you."

"Your daughter's very nice," I said.

Mrs. Mitford's brow slightly furrowed and she stepped closer and rested her hand on my arm. "The only thing is I do think you've been keeping her out a little late, and I wanted to ask you to get her home earlier, if you don't mind."

I didn't know what she was talking about.

"No, I don't mind."

"What do you think is fair?"

"What do you mean?"

"I mean, what time do you think is fair?" she elaborated, now squeezing my wrist. "I don't want to be too old-fashioned. I just think one o'clock is too late when you both have to work so hard the next day."

I looked directly into her eyes to see if I could see any signs of hardening of the arteries.

"What time do you think is good?" I asked.

"First of all, I don't think it's right for you to be taking her out so much. It must be costing you a great deal of money. You should make Della pay her share. I don't like her being spoiled."

"She's not spoiled. You really have a lovely offspring," I stressed.

"She said you're taking her to the Schroon Lake Drive-In tonight?"

"I was thinking about it," I mumbled. I really had no idea what she was talking about. Maybe she was on insulin. I didn't know.

"Well, I guess that'll get out pretty late, but as a rule I'd like her home by eleven or eleven-thirty, if you don't mind."

"No, I don't mind."

"You don't think I'm being unreasonable?"

"No, not at all.

"I guess Della's been pretty busy with Aunt Claire lately," I decided to plumb.

"Who?"

"Aunt Claire."

"Aunt Claire? My sister?"

"I understand you cooked a goose for her the other night."

"Oh, no. Claire's in Leningrad."

I was stunned. I disengaged my arm from her grasp and reached out to lean on a frozen-juice appliance.

"When did she go to Leningrad?"

"In May. She arrived May Day, when they have that grotesque tanks-and-missiles parade. She won't be back until Christmas. I don't know how she can bear it."

"Neither do I," I admitted, lifting my now cold, clammy hand to my forehead to ward off an incipient, severe anxiety attack.

Friday, August 23

A) TEENAGER SELLS MOM TO ARABS

B) NAIROBI HOUSEWIVES THREATEN HOME CHORES STRIKE

C) TWO-HEADED AUSTRALIAN BABY IS BOTH BOY AND GIRL

Rumanian National Holiday.

Oh, God, I've become a spy. Last night I was so depressed about what Mrs. Mitford had told me, it took me until after ten P.M. to finish setting up. Della didn't even look at me once. Mahatma asked me if I wanted to stop down to Indian House for a late snack, but I told him I was busy. All I did was go to Hairy Mary's and sit at the curve of the bar, where I could see out the front window past the Budweiser waterfall sign and up Della's street. Over the course of almost three hours I ordered one pizza, one Tab with a lemon twist, a baconburger, and seven shots of scotch with sodawater chasers. I made believe I was sipping the scotches but every time I had milked enough time out of one I poured it into an ashtray or a pot of plastic carnations near the jukebox. After a while, I couldn't stand being wedged in the crowd, and then I just stood right in the window with the flickering lights hurting my eyeballs. Close to one A.M. I got an attack of claustrophobia, paid my check and overtipped the bartender. He was nice enough not to ask my age, though I was prepared to tell him I was a midget.

Around ten minutes after one A.M. I was hiding behind the trunk of a major maple tree two houses down from 163 Hear Ye Road. At seventeen minutes to two a beat-up Ford pulled up precisely across the street from the tree. A boy with a crew cut was behind the wheel. Della was next to him. They necked for eight minutes. Then Della got out and ran up the street and went into her house. The Ford made a U-turn and headed back to Main Street.

Saturday, August 24

"Beauty of poppy conceals sting of death."—Charlie Chan.

> *To Ruth*
> *It is not the pen that*
> *writes friend,*

> But the friend that
> writes with the pen.
> Your classmate,
> Walter Hegge

Got letter from Calvin Kennedy. Here is text:

Dear Eugene, You Ace!

Was really glad to get your letter. Sorry it took me so long to write back. Bayonne is jumping. You don't know what you've missed this summer. Ha! Ha! I was thinking about you. Remember the time when you were over my house and we were up in my room and I had a bayonet and we were listening to the top hundred golden oldies on the radio and said if they played "Laughing on the Outside, Crying on the Inside" we'd each have to draw blood and write our names on the wall? Good thing it never played. Ha! Ha! There's been one party after the other after you left. I was glad you told me I hurt your feelings when I didn't get over to say goodbye because I said I had a fever but you saw me with Jake and Flick driving by. Sorry, pal. I really wish you were around for last night's party. I swear to God everyone ended up in their birthday suits at Clove Pond Park. First, I have to tell you about the thirty or forty parties before that. I've been drunk for almost two months straight. The first was at Norma Swick's house on Westerland Street. Her mother went to Cape Cod for a month to study gemology and take a course on how to moonlight with a personal computer. What a blast we had. Norma's father would be turning over in his grave if he saw half the bodies that rolled around on his shag rug.

You wouldn't recognize half the girls. They've all grown great melons except for Betty Roots who's get-

ting to look more like a hang glider. I really miss you, Ace. No kidding. Are you having a wild time up there? Where are you, exactly? Maybe one night when we're all drunk we'll drive up the Thruway and surprise you. You're missing so much down here. The only one whose parents didn't go away this summer is Rick O'Connor's and that's because Mr. O'Connor had a gallstone operation and fell off a ladder. We found keys to everybody's liquor cabinets and where they hid bottles in the cellars. There's no mothers or fathers around to cramp anybody's style. Mary Lou Zambo's mother decided to go to law school. Pat's father is attending a motorcycle mystery tour of the Poconos. We had three parties at Peggy Noggen's house because her mother has opened a catering business for fun and profit with her sister in Port Jervis.

I see your mother's dating again. I spoke to her on the phone, did she tell you? Who is that guy living with her? He looks like a chimpanzee. I see them in that neat Packard all the time. Sometimes when I see them go by it looks like your mother's hiding from me or else she's got a calcium deficiency. She's really a nice lady. Saturday nights I usually see them parked in the back of Baskin-Robbins 31 Flavors necking. Anyway, it's one big ball here. When are you coming home? Hurry. The summer's almost over. Between Jake, Flick, Andy, Rick, Ed Vogel, Norma, Betty Roots, Pat, Peggy, Barbara Johannsen and Mary Lou Zambo alone their folks are preoccupied with the fruits of their new interests which also include self-hypnosis, shiatsu, the Jack LaLanne Spas, aerobic karate, poker, package tours, courses in massage for couples, dating bloopers and blunders, understanding phobias, windsurfing, and how to reverse your credit. A lot of parents are also in triathlons and budget hot-air ballooning. Ha! Ha! We're having a blast, Eugene. Last night's party was another one at Norma Swick's. At least it started there. By midnight everyone was pretty stoned or making believe they were and we started playing some games that really freaked us out. We started with strip poker and spin-the-bottle. Those were just for laughs. But then we started playing the truth game where everyone had to take turns and say something they really felt was truthful from their hearts. The things people started saying became crazier and crazier and I was too drunk to really remember them but they were metaphysical and weird like the things you usually like to talk about, Ace. Ha! Ha! I think I told everyone I planned to become a priest. Things like that. There were just no rules to what any one of us wanted to say. No one cared. And then somehow we all ended up in Rick's van and we drove to Woodland Cemetery and started running past the graves all the way down to the start of Clove Pond Park. That was where I started to take off my clothes. First, I threw my shirt in the air and then my shoes and all the guys and girls started doing the same thing. We all ran down the big hill there and even Betty Roots took off her top. It was really a frenzy with melons and goobers bouncing all around. It wasn't even an orgy. It's like last night we all went even further than sex. We were mating with the moonlight. We were running as fast as we could and there was nothing left to stop us anymore. I had so much beer in me, I even began to believe there was no gravity. God, Ace, I wish you had been there!

I really feel badly about telling you I had a fever. I suppose you really deserve to know the truth or I wouldn't be a decent pal to you. When you called I really did *want to come over and say good-bye to you but Jake and Flick had already invited me to go cruising with them in the convertible. I asked them if I could invite you and they said they didn't want you. They think you're too square and I tried to tell them that you've got a great sense of humor. They also think you're a fruit. I tried to stick up for you but it just didn't work. They think you're too blond. They're really being very unfair, Ace. I think I can straighten everything out when you get back to Bayonne. I've already decided to teach you how to play softball better so the ball doesn't hit you on the head when you play left field. Also, I've decided you should start smoking cigars. Fruits don't smoke cigars and I think that'd really fix your image. Anyway, so long for now. Write soon. Your pal,*

Calvin

Saturday, August 24—Eleven more days until the hotel closes

I asked Della out this morning near the burnishing machine. She said she was really very sorry but she had to stay home because her aunt Claire was teaching her Parisian idioms. I knew she was lying, so every word she said cut into my heart like a knife. I just didn't know what to do to stop the pain.

Tonight I arrived at my maple tree at 11:12 P.M. At 12:37 A.M. a VW dropped Della off out of sight of Mrs. Mitford. The driver had a beard and looked like a lumberjack.

Sunday, August 25—Ten more days

I got to the maple at 11:02 P.M. At 11:45 P.M. a yellow Dodge coupe pulled up and let Della out. The driver looked like an egomaniacal abstract painter. I'm only exposing myself to more and more self-destructive pain, but I can't seem to stop myself. I woke up at three in the morning shaking with chills.

Monday, August 26

Arrived maple at 10:43 P.M. At 1:13 Della was dropped off in a Toyota truck by some brawny boy who looked like he made seashell jewelry.

Tuesday, August 27

1) **mel·lif·lu·ous** (mə-lif ′loo-əs) *adj*. Flowing with honey.
   Midnight—Bunker walked Della almost home.

Wednesday, August 28

"A little learning is a dang'rous thing."—Alexander Pope.

Elizabeth Seton, first American-born saint, born, 1774.

It takes one day to get a divorce in the Dominican Republic.

Got a letter from Laurette. Here is text:

Dear Eugene,

Your father was very glad to receive your note. He's muskie fishing today in the St. Lawrence with my brothers, Harold and Alex, but wanted me to respond to you on his behalf. He and I both appreciate your invitation. We're sure the Pine Knoll Motel is very lovely, but please don't make any reservation for us. A heated pool would certainly be a treat because we've only been swimming off the Thousand Islands, and as you can imagine none of the waters even remotely near Quebec are anything less than ice-cold. Of course, your father would very much like to see you, but our time is getting very cramped. My parents want us to stay here through Labor Day, which may be an impossibility. We hadn't told you because no plans were set until now, but your father and I will be flying to London for a two-month vacation on September 9th, so we must get back and pack as soon as possible. I think England is the most wonderful place on Earth, and I'm very excited about seeing fine theater and having high tea at Harrods.

At the moment we plan to leave Quebec City early on

September 3rd or 4th. You're only a couple of hundred miles from here, so it is possible we could route ourselves by your hotel and visit for an hour or two. However, we would have to continue directly on to Manhattan, as your father's eyes have grown very sensitive to headlights so we want to keep night driving to a minimum. According to the schedule you sent your father and me, I imagine the only possibility would be to arrive about 1:30 P.M. If we can't make it please forgive us. We will definitely get together in New York in the fall sometime. I know you'd like as much time with your father as possible. At least you'll get a postcard of Big Ben and a Beefeater or raven.

Sincerely,
Laurette

3 P.M.—*Still Wednesday*

I came back from lunch so depressed I threw up and put away any other half-read books, and started reading *Moby-Dick* by Herman Melville. The opening grabbed me right away: "Call me Ishmael. Some years ago— never mind how long precisely—having little or no money in my purse, and nothing particular to interest me on shore, I thought I would sail about a little and see the watery part of the world. . . ."

It made me think of me on the lake, although this guy's on an ocean. It's a pretty thick book and I know I'll soon be hooked by it and will forget my depression for a while.

"Like Narcissus," Mr. Melville writes, "all of us see in the ocean the image of the ungraspable phantom of life."

I read all the way as far as where Ishmael has to share his bed with a harpooner named Queequeg who proves to be not very talkative but civil and they smoke a tomahawk-shaped pipe together and worship some idol. Right around this point I felt unexplainably scared.

11:43 P.M.—Still Wednesday

I want to die. I feel so terrible. Forgive me, Dear Diary, but I'm in awful pain. I know it's not very brave for a boy to cry into his soup, but I made a deal to be honest here. It's got to be okay for a person to let himself know he's crying in his own soup. Anyway, I can't help myself after what has happened tonight. I came home right from the dining room and swore I would just stay in and read *Moby-Dick*. Then around 10:30 I told myself it'd be better if I just took *Moby-Dick* with me and read it out in the fresh air.

I read on the dormitory porch for five minutes and decided the lighting wasn't right and that there was a bright night light outside the zoo door that would be just right and I could see the lake from there.

It was all only my subconscious leading me on, I finally had to realize, because as I got closer to the hotel I knew very well tonight was the weekly staff show.

I didn't even make an attempt to read any more and just carried the book with me around the left-wing annex and joined the rest of the employees who were watching the show. By the time I got to the spot on the lawn there were the usual waiters, bellhops, and captains peering into the nightclub, and the show was already underway with Huey up on the two chairs manipulating the little Fred Astaire and Ginger Rogers marionettes to "Puttin' on the Ritz."

The sight of Huey still turned my stomach.

Alfredo and Louie were hustling the crowd for tips as usual and smiling at everyone.

Next Zola sang "My World May Be Lonely But I Will Wait for You" particularly well, I thought—and then came the bartender who sang "Ave Maria" and "Let's Get Physical," and he did an encore, which was "Material Girl." I didn't really listen to any of it. All I could think of was Della.

Huey tonight had the Rockette marionettes do "You're a Grand Old Flag" forever, but finally Della and her backup waitresses were in the spotlight. She had borrowed a *mink* stole from one of the guests tonight, and everyone went silent again as she sang:

> . . . *Oh, my heart belongs to Daddy,*
> *Da da da, da da da,*
> *Da da da . . .*

When Della finished, everyone applauded even more than the first time I'd seen the show.

Then Captain Pegeen and the salad chef began executing their "Orchids in the Moonlight" tango.

During this Della and her backups came out the side door as usual to accept the plaudits of the staff on the lawn. Tonight there was no Bunker around nor Mahatma nor any of his Indian pals for that matter.

I was able to reach Della.

I could tell she had seen me coming out of the corner of her eye, and I waited until she had received her last plaudit before speaking to her.

"That was really good," I said matter-of-factly.

"Thank you," she said coldly.

"Della, I need to talk to you."

"I can't."

"Just a few minutes."

"I'm sorry."

"Is Bunker here?"

"No, he's not."

"Can I walk you home?"

"I have to wait for the curtain call."

"After that, can I walk you home?"

"My mother's waiting for me."

"Your aunt Claire, too?" I threw in. "Tonight she wants you to help make squid meatballs?"

Della looked surprised for a moment, then she made believe she was looking at the moon. "As a matter of fact, yes," she said.

I hated myself for being sarcastic, but I felt so hurt.

"Just let me walk you as far as Main Street, please," I asked softly, almost pleading.

She paused.

"If you want to."

"I'll wait for you down at the bridge," I said. Then Huey was out screaming for all cast members to line up inside for the curtain call.

Della nodded okay, then disappeared through the doorway.

Della took about forty-five minutes before she met me on the bridge, and we walked slowly along Skunks Misery Lane toward Loudon's Landing. The moon had gone behind a cloud, and it was very dark and depressing.

"What do you want?" she asked before we had passed the Buzz-Ro-All driveway.

"I was wondering who you go out with," I said.

"What are you talking about?"

"I mean, you told me you saw Bunker once in a while, but I was wondering if you were seeing anyone else."

"Well, all that should matter is whether I'm seeing you or not."

"But I don't get to go out with you. All you tell me is you have to make baked ziti with your aunt Claire."

"Don't you want me to see my aunt?"

"I wouldn't mind that."

"Then, what's the problem?"

"Your mother told me your aunt is in Leningrad, Russia."

"Oh."

"Is she?"

"When did you see my mother?"

"In town last week."

"I see."

"I've seen you going out with a lot of guys."

"A lot?"

"Besides Bunker, I saw you kissing Louie and all sorts of guys dropping you off near your house."

"So, you've been spying on me?"

"I just needed to know what was going on."

"You felt you had that right?"

"You've been telling your mother you're going out with me so she won't know about the creeps you're really seeing. I saw you drive up with a Neanderthal in a Ford. And someone in a yellow Dodge who looks like he works in acrylics.''

"Look, Eugene . . ."

"Just please try to explain it to me. Please."

"Look, I don't have to give you any excuses for where I go at night. I hardly know you. We went out once in a canoe and I had you over for *café au lait* and madeleines. That was it."

"We see each other every day in the dining room."

"I see a lot of people in the dining room."

"But I told you how I felt in my heart."

"I don't have to give you any explanations."

"I think you do."

"I've had many friends before I met you, and I still have friends. You don't have any hold on me. You can't tell me what to do."

"I thought you were more selective."

"Well, who are you to tell me how selective I am? I'm very selective."

"I'm sorry, but I don't think the collection of Neanderthals I've seen you with are great selections. I don't understand. I know I'm only a waiter, but I know they don't talk about Simone de Beauvoir and Jean-Paul Sartre."

"Well, it's none of your business what they talk about."

"I told you my deepest-most feelings. I trusted you with them. I bared my soul to you and you haven't acted the same to me since. You act like you don't even want to see me, much less talk to me. I think it's only my goose that's been getting cooked. I don't understand. I think I deserve more honesty than that."

"Well . . ."

"Please don't just keep saying 'Well . . .' "

"Eugene, if it's honesty you want, I'll give it to you. I'm not living my life just for you. I've known a lot of boys and men before you came here, and I'll know a lot more after you're gone. I go out every night because I don't want to stay home. What does it matter to you?"

"How can you ask that after what I've confessed to you?"

"You really expect me to go into that?"

"Can you at least tell me if you're being intimate with all these goons?"

"I don't have to answer that question. All you have to know is I'm not being intimate with you."

"Oh, that hurts. That hurts me very much."

"Do I ask you who you're being intimate with?"

"I told you I was a virgin," I reminded her.

"You could also tell me you're the King of Prussia. Does any of it really matter? Virginity isn't for everyone, you know."

"You really are making love with the sort of people whose fathers own monkey farms?

"I'm not going to answer that."

"But what's wrong with me? Why don't you love me?"

"Why? I'll tell you why. Because you seem to have skipped a few steps in what normal people do when they form a relationship."

"For instance. Just give me a couple of for instances."

"You're stuck in some kind of fantasy world."

"Writers are supposed to be."

"I'm sorry, but even for writers there's no such thing as marriage at first sight. You're supposed to go more slowly. You can't tell a girl what you told me without freaking her out."

"I freaked you out?"

"Of course you did."

"What should I have done?"

"You should have taken it slower. We'd have had a start and seen if it lasted a while. Then we'd first be friends. And after a much longer time if we became physical with each other then we'd start thinking about a remote possibility of really focusing in on each other. That would take a long time. And then normal people talk about marriage. I don't think about marrying *anyone* yet. Nobody normal my age does. In terms of this summer, we don't even know each other."

"I do have a big fantasy about you."

The moon peeked out from behind a cloud, so I could really see she was holding her head like I was driving her crazy.

"You had no right to think I was going to jump into a wedding with you."

"All I can say is I did it the only way I knew how. I didn't know any other way to let you know my feelings except to tell them to you."

"Well, you jumped."

We were getting very close to the lights on Main Street, and I began to panic about time running out.

"Then what's in the future for us?" I blurted sincerely.

"What are you talking about?"

"Labor Day is practically here. Do you see any possibilities for us?"

"Do you write letters?"

"Yes."

"Then can't we write to each other? Maybe we could even see each other if I ever came down to New York.

147

We could see a French farce or go to a museum and see an Impressionist exhibit, perhaps.''

''You wouldn't want to make an arrangement now, would you?''

''You mean like pinpoint it to five-fifteen on November seventeenth or something?''

''Yes. Plan it,'' I suggested.

''Plan it? Do you have a calendar in your head ready or something like that?''

''We write it down.''

''Isn't that compulsive?''

''But isn't setting a day necessary?''

''What if we pick a day and then one of us finds when the day gets closer there's something more important we have to do like get pneumonia or have a root canal? We might plan a date in February or March and by then we might not even want to see each other, and we're all marked down in ink.''

''You don't like the idea.''

''No. Where's the flow of it? What if I'm busy that month?''

We had reached Loudon's Landing, and its lights washed over us. Unfortunately, they also washed over someone else I could see waiting, leaning against a railing on the corner.

It was Bunker.

''Good night, Eugene,'' Della said, as though ordering me to halt my feet and let her continue toward Bunker.

''Just a few more minutes,'' I pleaded.

''No.''

I walked on with her, staying right at her side until Bunker turned from the railing and stood in front of us.

"Snooks bothering you?" Bunker asked.

"No," Della said, taking Bunker's hand and walking on a few steps with him in tow.

I halted at the corner.

"Please, Della," I said.

Bunker let go of her hand and started walking back to me.

"Don't go near him," Della ordered protectively of me.

"I won't touch him," Bunker said calmly.

Bunker moved his face close to mine, completely blocking out Della in the background. We were right under one of the streetlights now, and the rays fell down making his face look monstrous. His eyes were black holes and his cheeks looked like death. He looked like a Matt Dillon disembodied smiling skull.

"Now, Snooks," he whispered so it'd be our own private little secret. "I've warned you before but this is your last chance. I don't even want to catch you breathing near Della again."

"Or what?" I asked.

"Or I'll press your face on a hot waffle iron."

"Oh."

"And one other thing, Snooks. If I catch you out on the lake again, I'll drown you." He added sweetly, "You understand that, Snooks? Do you?"

Bunker let the smile completely fade from his face, and he looked like a complete gorgon as he strode back to Della. They disappeared up Hear Ye Road.

Thursday, August 29

"Nine-tenths of people are created so you would want to be with the other tenth."—Horace Walpole

A) BAG LADY ESCAPES JAWS OF DEATH IN TRASH COMPACTOR
B) LOST BOY FOUND ASLEEP IN ARMS OF FIVE-HUNDRED-POUND GORILLA
C) LAWYER FORCES PREGNANT WIFE TO CARRY HIM PIGGYBACK

Sent special-delivery letter to Dad. Text as follows:

Dear Dad:

I received Laurette's letter sent on your behalf. I hope you caught a muskie. I'm very happy you and Laurette are going to England, but Dad, I very much need you to stop by on your drive back to New York. I am in trouble and need to talk to you very much. I am so depressed I can't wait until the fall like Laurette mentioned. I find myself thinking of suicide. I would never really kill myself, don't worry about that. It's only my subconscious that has been considering putting a dry cleaner's bag over my head. I don't need money. I need to know what's wrong with me. There are pieces missing from me. From my mind. I think it's because I don't really know you. I've never been around you long enough to learn things I should know by now. I have no eye-hand coordination. I think that's because you were too busy working as a cop to throw a baseball or football with me, and when you moved out there was no

*chance for me to learn anything from you at all. I
don't know how to love. I don't even know how I should
feel about sex. My mind works all the time, but it only
makes blueprints which have nothing to do with my
emotions. I lied to you when I told you I was doing a lot
of aquatic sports. I only wanted to be something you
wouldn't be ashamed of. I know you were a football
hero in high school and swam to Ellis Island from
Hoboken as a lark with buddies and that you earned all
those sharpshooter medals at the police academy. I'm
so proud of you, Dad. But can you help me? Just talk to
me. I think a lot of sons go all the way through life
without ever really getting to know their fathers, but
please make a start with me. I hope this letter isn't
embarrassing you. I hope Laurette isn't angry I'm
mentioning these things. You don't even have to stay
overnight at the Pine Knoll Motel, but if I could only
know you'll be stopping by for an hour. I'll look for you
every day from here on in from 1:30 P.M. on, in case
you decide to drive down a day or two early. I need to
know all the different kinds of love and how I can find
the happiness that belongs to me. I need to know if
there's any God I should really believe in. I'm not
blaming you for anything. Everything is my fault. I
just don't know where to begin to fix myself. Is it
just because I have a teenage brain? Is it because
there's some incurable separation between the left
side of my brain and my right side? I'm frightened,
Dad. I don't like myself. I've been trying but it's not
working. Please stop by. I won't be any trouble. Please
let me talk to you alone. This is not to offend Laurette,
who is wonderful. I need you now. I'll be waiting. I
love you so much and I only know my missing pieces*

*have something to do with you. Help me, please.
Mom tried playing catch with me but she wasn't very
good.*

> *Your loving son,
> Eugene*

Friday, August 30

I'm too depressed to write.

Saturday, August 31

Caligula born, A.D. 12.
  "In spite of everything I still believe that people are
really good at heart."—Anne Frank
  A) MARILYN MONROE'S GHOST APPEARS TO SENATE
     PAGE
  B) SPITEFUL LADY DENTIST PULLS OUT HUSBAND'S
     GIRLFRIEND'S TEETH
  C) MERMAID COLONY SIGHTED OFF LIVERPOOL

Dear Diary,
  I feel like I'm trapped in a movie. A movie that is
coming to an end. My summer is over Wednesday,
September 4—two days after the Lake Henry Hotel's
gala Labor Day celebration. That's only four days

152

away! I'm desperate. I have so many things to finish by then:

a) My Dad will stop by. I can feel it in my heart.

b) I'll have to say good-bye to Mahatma. I hope he doesn't feel I've been avoiding him.

c) I can't leave without Della knowing how much I really love her and that we're definitely destined for each other.

d) Do I really have to go home to my mattress that Charlie Mayo has been sleeping on?

e) Am I going back to Bayonne at all? Am I going to continue to live with my mother, who's taking all of her orders from Gail Sheehy?

f) Penelope will be going back to New Paltz. I love her so much, and the whole summer's gone by without us really being together. She's my only real, real friend who cares about me, besides Mahatma. I won't see her for a long time. At least I'll be able to offer her some money to help with college.

g) Please tell me, Dear Diary—do diaries ever really come to an end? I feel just so sad and drowning in at least thirty-three mysteries about my life and I don't know if you're going to be able to help me as much as I thought you would. Mysteries are supposed to be solved, aren't they? I don't know if I have enough red blood corpuscles left to find all the answers. My soul feels like trolls, gnomes, a Minotaur, and a thousand horrors of haute cuisine have been jumping on it trying to wear it down.

h) Intellectuals are supposed to try to catch humanity in their teeth. Please help me not back away as I face these final hours of my pubescence.

i) Is logic taking over my flesh and blood? I can't let

it. I must fight it. I don't want to end up as just one more suburban roarer.

j) I don't really believe now that there is going to be a death or marriage to wind up this summer. Nothing in real life is that tidy. I wanted to have you go one way, Dear Diary, but then you keep going another. I pray at least I'll be carried to some exciting goal I cannot foresee from my present depressed state. I feel like one of Della's geese trying to lay a huge square egg. I don't know what happens to a goose that tries such a thing. It probably dies.

k) And one more thing, Dear Diary. Don't let me lie to you.

Sunday, September 1

Mr. Micci stiffed me four dollars again.

I am lonely and miserable. I wanted to rent a canoe and go out on the lake but I don't dare. Maybe I am a coward and a fruit.

I waited down by the bridge from 1:23 to 4:38 but didn't see my father or his maroon Chrysler New Yorker with power windows.

At 4:39 I saw Mahatma come to the door of Indian House and wave to me. I decided to go sit on a log with him where I could still see if Dad and Laurette drove onto the island. He began to interrogate me straight off.

"You look like you've lost a lot of weight," he said. "Why haven't you come to see me?"

"I have problems," I said.

"The waitress with the ponytail doesn't even look at you anymore."

I decided to just ignore that astute observation.

"I'm waiting for my father. He's stopping by on his way down from Canada," I let him know.

"When?" Mahatma sounded very excited for me.

"Any day now. How's Shiva?"

"Good. I polished him up this morning. I'll tell him you asked for him."

I could tell from Mahatma's tone he knew I was shutting him out. I really didn't want him to feel that way. "Listen, I wanted to let you know I really appreciated you being nice to me," I told him. "You and all the Buddha and Hindu guys. You're really very nice people. I'm sorry I didn't get to know you better."

"Are you?"

"Yes, I am."

He linked his laser eyes into mine.

"I don't think you are. I offered to tell you answers to many mysteries, and you only found out about reversal and then never came back to see me. You never came back because you didn't like what you heard. What *is* really bothering you now?" he asked, sounding really concerned.

"I can only be general," I said.

"Okay."

"I'm not talking about Della."

"Shoot."

"I just need to know what makes a pretty girl go out with a lot of ugly guys."

"How many?"

"Lots."

"That answer is easy," he said almost with anger. "She's a reprobate. A snake."

"She's not a snake."

"In India she'd be considered a very evil snake. In the United States you'd say she has the evil of Adam's girlfriend in her."

"Eve?" I asked.

"Yes. This girl is as evil as Eve was in the Bible. She's without morals. She doesn't seek out godly things."

"But she looks like an angel."

"She's a snake."

"Maybe she just doesn't know any better. Maybe no one ever really taught her the difference between bad and good. Maybe she had no father or an obsessive mother. Maybe she comes from an insane background like me."

"Ignorance is no excuse."

"How can you say things like that? Now you know why I don't come around very much," I said. I was getting just as emotional as he was.

"The only thing you hate is truth. I told you when you see a harlot, cross the street. That's the safest thing."

"But I don't want to cross the street. I want her to love me."

"But you told me she loves only ugly guys. You're not ugly."

"Why does she go out with them?"

"You said she's an angel. Well, some angels always seek the opposite. Many people are like that. They're angels who want devils."

"But I think she really tries hard to be a good angel."

"She's still a harlot."

"She knows a lot of French."

"She's learned French but no morality. She looks around and always wants to try something different. If she's in your path and you must come face to face with her you should grab her by her shoulders and shake her."

"Shake her?"

"Yes. You shake her and you yell, COME OUT OF THIS GIRL, YOU DEMON!"

"But I love her," I muttered.

"Of course you do," Mahatma almost shouted. "You're a snake too." Then he poked me with his knuckles.

"I'm a snake?"

"You're a big reprobate, too. A big, big, wicked snake."

"I am not."

"Who are you kidding? You have no morality either."

"I'm fifteen."

"So? You're a fifteen-year-old viper."

"Look, I'm trying my best to love someone."

"You lie to yourself!"

"I do not. If you're so smart, tell me what love really is," I demanded. "You said I'd have to love myself first. Then you twirl your hands in a circle and tell me the secret of life is reversal. Well, I like myself now," I lied. "I not only like me, I think I love me. I just don't know what love really is."

Mahatma gave me another punctuation with his knuckles and made his circle gesture.

"Love of your father is true love. Love of your mother, too. Love of a friend, too. Love without question. That is love. Right now you're an unenlightened teenage boy, but soon you'll know all this. I see in your eyes one day you'll get high scores on S.A.T. tests."

"But how can I learn to love?" I asked.

"It's a bad time for that in this country and lots of other places.

"Why?"

"Too many people are ignorant of their need. Everybody thinks they can get along without love or honesty. It's a very big horror."

I didn't say anything for a moment. Finally, I could get my lips moving again.

"I don't think I can get along," I said weakly.

"You're a snake trying to change your skin."

"How can I change faster?"

"Love and honesty must be learned. There's no magic way."

"Learned from who?"

"From parents. From grandmothers. From uncles and books. From somebody. From an old Hindu who smells of curry."

Monday, September 2—Two days left

It's Labor Day.

in•iq•ui•tous•ly (**i-nik´wə-təs-lē**) *adv*. Wickedly, unjustly.

Hitler invades Poland, 1939—starts World War II.

"Punish my sons, when they grow up, O judges, paining them as I have pained you, if they appear to you to care for riches or anything else before virtue. And if they think themselves to be something when they are nothing, reproach them as I have done you."—Socrates, before drinking his poison.

A) MONK CRUISES OVER NIAGARA FALLS IN BLESSED BARREL
B) CHUBBY NUN DIES BY MISTAKE IN FAT-FARM HORROR
C) GRANDFATHER, 87, MAKES DEATHBED WISH TO BE BURIED IN PINK PARTY DRESS

Afternoon Entry: 2:17 P.M.— While waiting at the bridge

There is a great tension building over the big gala tonight. Alfredo and Louie are dealing like crazy already, making the nightclub reservations and lining up their final gratuities of the summer. Everybody is thinking about their tips, because check-out is Wednesday and guests will have to prorate gratuities, remembering the 25 cents for breakfast, 25 cents for lunch, and 50 cents for dinner. I'm thinking of stopping Mr. Micci in the lobby when he pays his bill and telling him politely he's inadvertently stiffed me four dollars a week for over eight weeks.

Thank God I've already saved a thousand dollars. Am worried about how I'll withdraw it and carry it back to Bayonne. I don't expect Mr. Micci's table to give me a season bonus, but the laxative table has been very responsive to extra service I've given them. I've gotten so used to the strange undercurrents at their table. I still think there's been too much genetic familiarity and a few of them wear their hair very strangely, especially Sonny Ex-Lax. I think they're close friends of the Du Ponts.

My stag table has changed so many times none of the original look-alikes remain except Princess Di, Twiggy, and a Brat Packer type. The other seven I've had for over two weeks, and they look like W. Somerset Maugham, Mamie Eisenhower, Mao Tse-tung, a Pointer Sister, Mother Teresa, Edna St. Vincent Millay, and Cher.

I asked Della by her picture window if I could talk to her more. She said no.

Two other distressing things happened at lunch. One was with Cher's coffee and the other involved a steak for Edna St. Vincent Millay. Cher complained to me her coffee was always too cold. I apologized and poured her a fresh cup from the aluminum pot on the electric heater at my tray table. It was very hot, and I rushed it to her but she said it was still too cold. At that moment

Captain Pegeen smelled a way to milk a side tip out of Cher and remind the rest of the table of all the special niceties she's performed.

"I'll give you a lovely cup of extra-hot coffee," Captain Pegeen assured Cher.

Captain Pegeen signaled me to follow her to the kitchen and whispered she wanted me to know all the tricks of serving truly hot, hot coffee. To make a long story short, first she took an individual clay teapot and rinsed it with hot water from a giant aluminum heater, then dumped the water out and quickly filled it with hot coffee from the main coffee urn. Then she ran with the hot coffee in the hot coffeepot straight out to the Cher look-alike and poured it right in front of her, vapors and all. Cher sipped it and said it wasn't hot enough.

"Oh?" Captain Pegeen said, surprised. She said she'd fix it for sure now, and this time she ran out into the kitchen, grabbed a cup, saucer and clay pot and really let the scalding water fall all over them. Then she filled the pot with hot coffee, covered everything with a towel and really ran back to the table. Cher sipped and said it was okay, but not as hot as she would like it.

"We aim to please," Captain Pegeen said. "We'll make you happy yet."

Captain Pegeen then ran back out to the kitchen. This time she first took a cup and placed it facing down on a metal grill in the broiler section. As the cup heated she went through the hot water routine with the saucer, clay pot and even a spoon, then filled the pot with boiling coffee. She put the stuff on a tray, ran back to the cup on the grill, and you could actually see the brim had begun to turn white-hot. Now she delivered a cup of coffee that looked like it had been forged in hell. When Cher lifted the cup to her mouth I heard her lower lip sear.

"That *is* lovely," Cher said, and Captain Pegeen beamed and gave me a wink.

The second distressing thing that happened at lunch involved Edna St. Vincent Millay's steak entrée. When I served it to her she used a steak knife and said the meat was too tough. I told her I'd let the broiler chef know, and took it back to the kitchen. There was a long line for steaks, but when it was my turn again I told the broiler chef the guest complained the meat was too tough. Bunker was assisting the steak line and he winked at the broiler chef and said, "Fix it up good for Snooks."

"Sure," the chef said.

Then he took Edna St. Vincent Millay's steak off the plate, dropped it on the floor, and stomped on it with the heel of his right foot. He picked it up in a flash, brushed it with melted butter and put it right back on the plate and handed it to me.

"It's nice and tender now," the chef said, and Bunker laughed.

I said, "Thank you," took the steak back out to the dining room and threw it onto a garbage tray. Then I went back to the kitchen and got on line and ordered a new steak like it was for another guest.

Midnight—The Labor Day Gala
is over

A terrible thing happened. I'm very depressed. It's worse than the steak.

The gala started easy enough. It was a set menu, which meant everybody got the same food. First they got a fruit cup in a parfait glass that was wrapped in blue cellophane and tied with a silver rubber band. Then they got vichyssoise for the next course. Then they got an intermezzo of a tiny dish of lemon sherbet and a small course of fillet of sole. Then they got a big broiled lobster. Then the lights were put out in the dining room and the band, the spruced-up kitchen workers, and the waiters and waitresses all lined up outside while they jammed lighted sparklers into dozens of white ice cream cakes called Bombes Glacés. Each waiter carried one for his station, and the head chef in his white puffed hat and red cheeks led the band and us in a march into the dining room. The band played "When the Saints Come Marching In," and everybody screamed and yelled and celebrated at the sight of all the marching trumpets and ignited ice cream cakes. After one march around the dining room, Alfredo signaled us all to disband and rush with our cakes to our stations, where the captains were waiting with special knives and hot water to cut the cakes. It was really a very thrilling spectacle, something like I imagine they must do at only the best hotels in Nassau and St.

Tropez. Three unfortunate things happened during the march.

1) I was so busy trying to stay close to Della in line I tripped and almost dropped my Bombe Glacé.

2) Bunker blew a mock kiss at me and mouthed "Snooks."

3) Mr. Micci got into a fight with Maître d' Alfredo and called him a Cuban commie spic.

Mr. Micci said it so loudly and viciously everyone in the dining room heard it. The place went really silent and a lot of people looked, probably to see if Alfredo was going to plunge a butter knife into him or not. I could see the split second of hate that crossed Alfedo's face, and I thought he might at least strike with a spatula. Instead, Alfredo suddenly smiled, signaled the band to keep playing and charmed Mr. Micci so that everything looked smoothed over. The gala went back into full party gear, and it wasn't until later I found out what had happened. It seems Mr. Micci wanted to reserve a special front table at the nightclub and Alfredo wanted to get a tip for it and Micci wouldn't go for it. Mr. Micci also had had too much to drink. Anyway, even though the invective Mr. Micci used was really ugly, Alfredo acted like he had forgiven everything and gave Mr. Micci the table he wanted without a tip.

Tuesday, September 3—The most gross and horrendous day

1) Emily Post born, 1873.

Dear Diary,

I am writing this in you from a shocking and unexpected place. I can't even bring myself to write down where I am because I'm still psychically paralyzed. I have given all of today's events very careful thought and I've seriously considered lying to you. But I can't. Diaries must be truthful. That was the one rule I accepted before I even started writing here. What I didn't realize was things would happen to me at this summer's end that would be so painful I would do anything to change them. However, then I'd have a fictitious diary, and that sounds like a literary impossibility and a cheat to myself. It wasn't until now that I came up with a solution that can make my forthcoming and final confession bearable. After somber contemplation I think I'll be able to record the whole truth and nothing but the truth if I do it mostly backward. No matter how I slice it, there are six confessions I must make in all, and I'm giving them special titles so I don't forget them.

a) "My Last Words with Della"
b) "My Mother's Shocking Letter"
c) "My Father's Visit"
d) "Something for Shiva, or, Farewell to Mahatma"
e) "My Death-Defying but Stupid Victory"
f) "A Prune Juice for Mr. Micci"

Actually, now that I've made a list of the events, I realize it's a bit like an emotional menu. The entire summer has been gastronomically related.

The first event I can record is my mother's letter. I didn't get that until I got to town after most of the other stuff had already gone down. The text follows:

Dear Eugene,

By the time you get this letter I will probably be in Atlanta or Virginia Beach. Our final destination is Orlando, Fla., where we will see Shamu, ride the scenic railway on Space Mountain, and do Epcot.

I know this letter will surprise you, but when you come home I won't be there. Charlie and I won't be back until October, and even then you won't have to worry about him sleeping in your bed. He'll be sleeping in mine. We are being married today in Havre de Grace, Maryland. We checked, and they do very quick nuptials there. I don't really care what you think about it because I know it's the right thing for me. You know my sister's son Eddie? He was still living with her when he was 26, so she went out one day to the Sopher Apartment Sales Agency and came home to let him know he had three months to find his own place, because she was selling the house and moving into a studio with river view in TriBeCa. Frankly, it was while reading The Female Eunuch *that I realized what I was going to do. You can go on loving your father and thinking he's going to suddenly change into a warm, loving, decent and responsible man and come home, but that's not in the cards. Your father is rotten and has damaged our lives and the sooner you get that through your head the better. Charlie wants to be a father to you if you'd like. I told him you wouldn't, but maybe your working for a change has helped your attitude. I spoke to Aunt Ruth and she said she can get you a job anytime. I love you, but grow up, will you?*

I'll think of you when I'm at Disney World and bring you home a Stuckey's Pecan Log. I'm a bit nervous about being a bride again. But I'm very, very happy.

> *Love to you,*
> *Mom (the future Mrs.*
> *Charles Mayo)*

P.S. *I've already done your whole room with Lysol spray disinfectant and Airwick.*

Next I'll have to tell you about Mr. Micci's prune juice. Without that none of the other things would have happened, at least not in exactly the same way. This was the terrible thing which started the morning right off. I'm not ashamed of this part so much as sick to my stomach. I ate at the zoo and then went upstairs to check my station. It was only a few minutes to eight and the other waiters and waitresses were sleepwalking around the dining room football field. Alfredo was at the maître d' desk and I noticed him heading all the way back toward me, which was unusual right there. He usually made Louie check the worst stations.

"Good morning, Eugene," he said.

He looked well pomaded and distinguished in a powder-blue morning tux jacket with white pants, and his voice was smooth and mellifluous as usual. He didn't look very awake, but he definitely was one of the most kind and gracious Cuban persons I've ever met. I really thought he'd been a very dynamic and fair boss all summer.

"Hi," I said.

He stopped at my table of four. "This is where Mr. Micci sits?" he inquired, touching the back of one of the wooden chairs.

"Yes," I said.

"Eugene, when he comes in for breakfast just let me know what kind of juice he orders." He kept complete eye contact with me.

"Yes, sir."

Then he casually walked back to his maître d' desk and I started to feel strange. All I could remember was Mr. Micci calling Alfredo names the night before, and I decided maybe there was merely going to be some kind of change of tables or something. I guess my ears did start to tingle a bit from nerves, because on some level I figured there was something iniquitously wrong.

At 8:17 Mr. Micci, looking especially like A. Onassis with a faint hangover, came in for breakfast with the Jackie Kennedy, Sir Laurence Olivier, and Whoopi Goldberg lookalikes. For openers they ordered one prune, one orange, one cranapple, and one grapefruit juice. I took my tray and hurried toward the kitchen doors. I was thankful Alfredo wasn't at his desk at that moment, and I decided he had totally forgotten about the matter. Where he was, was waiting for me at the juice pick-up. As I set up my supremes Alfredo asked which juice was for Mr. Micci. I told him the prune, as I put a lemon wedge next to it. He tore the top off a small foil packet and dumped its contents of white powder into Mr. Micci's juice. He took a spoon and stirred it until the powder completely dissolved. Now I was extremely frightened, and my ankles started to shake.

"What is that?" I asked about the powder.

"A pachyderm emetic," Alfredo said calmly and scientifically.

"What's it for?"

"To make elephants throw up." He winked at me and added, "Now serve it."

I had all the juices on my tray now but my heart began pounding. I didn't know what to do. I took a step but then set the tray down.

"What'll it do?" I asked.

"Just don't expect to see Mr. Micci show up for lunch or dinner, and probably tomorrow's breakfast."

Alfredo set his panther eyes on me. I picked up the tray again and went out to the dining room. I walked very slowly toward my station. Of all the horrible things that had happened to me this was the most short-circuiting for my mind. I felt like I was now being pulled down into something genuinely evil. It was much worse than someone spitting on kiwis or stamping on Edna St. Vincent Millay's steak. I began to lose all coordination. I felt sick about the human race. Most of the other meanness I'd ever come across in my life was almost understandable. Now I was caught completely by surprise. I had never even thought about elephants sometimes needing a medicine to make them throw up, much less anyone wanting to give Mr. Micci one. He was stiffing me, that was true. And he had called Alfredo a really lousy name the night before. But all of this was out of my league. It was disillusioning and demoralizing.

I started to serve everyone else's juices first, and all I

could think of was something I'd once read about elephants. It was an article about how scientists think elephants have the ability to conceive of death. I'd read about it in the fifth grade. Elephants were known to seize the tusks from a dead member of the family and smash them to pieces. In Uganda when they kill elephants to cut down their numbers they store the ears and feet of the destroyed elephants in a shed to be prepared for sale as handbags and umbrella stands. But a group of elephants broke into the shed, removed all the dead parts and buried them one night. The book said the scientists were very uncomfortable about the event. That's exactly how I felt now—very uncomfortable.

When it came time to serve Mr. Micci I just left his juice at my tray stand and went up to Alfredo at his desk.

"I'm not going to do it," I told him.

"Then you're fired," he said nicely.

"I'm what?" I inquired.

"Fired. Pack your things and get off the island immediately." Then he just looked right past me and told Louie to serve the prune juice.

I couldn't speak. Louie escorted me to the kitchen doors and told me to get out. It wasn't even nine o'clock and it was all over. I'd lose my tips for the week. I'd lose any chance for a bonus from the laxative table. And poor Mr. Micci wouldn't be showing up for lunch or dinner, at least.

Once out in the kitchen I walked in a daze for the exit.

I saw Della picking up a fried haddock from Bunker at the grill.

I saw Mahatma.

I think Mahatma even spoke to me.

I just continued like a zombie down the exit stairs past the burnishing machine and out the zoo doors.

I headed back to the dormitory to pack.

Dear Diary, the next part of what happened to me hurts me so much I can't write it down yet. I'll tell you before I'm finished but not just now. I have to pretend what happened on my way to the dorm didn't happen for now. Let's just say that when I got back to the dormitory porch Mrs. Brady was sweeping and gave me a package. She also told me the dining room had called and said I was to pack and be off the island as soon as possible. I at least have to tell you what was in the package, because you'd never guess. It was a Willowcross shortwave radio receiver. Let's just say it really surprised me. I had never thought about a Willowcross shortwave radio in my life any more than I had ever thought about elephants getting emetics. I had never even heard of one. All I can say right now is the moment I opened the box in my room I learned I had become the owner of a Willowcross shortwave radio receiver. There was a note with it. I can't bear to record the text yet. The radio was black with silver dials and a glass front, which indicated six bands of stations located throughout the whole world, including Germany, Yugoslavia, China, Russia, Liechtenstein, Australia, England, the Fiji Islands, Canada, Mexico, Madagascar, and Tasmania. I laid a big sheet of instructions that came with it out on my bed and started packing. The Willowcross was only about a foot long, six inches wide and eight inches high. The instructions were more than a yard square, and showed all the aerial wires I'd need to hook up to get all the stations. I needed something like sixty feet of wire stretched in a northwest direction and thirty-three feet of wire stretched south and a rotating antenna sticking up into the sky and a grounding wire and a couple of other things that didn't even come in the box. I'd really need someone to show me how to do it, and even if I did manage to hook up all the wires in Bayonne, I'd have to beg half the neighbors' permissions to anchor everything to their houses. I could just see me sitting in Bayonne listening to the top hits from Borneo, news programs from the Yukon, and Antarctica's favorite call-in show. My first instinct was to just leave the Willowcross off at Indian House for Mahatma, but I finally decided to just pack it along with my worn-out clothes and revolting waiter's outfits. I knew I was too emotional at this point to make any sensible decision. Somebody had left a price tag on the Willowcross letting me know it cost eighty-seven dollars.

When I finished packing, Mrs. Brady told me she had to check my room to make sure I wasn't stealing any valuables that belonged to the dormitory. The only things possible to rip off would be the tattered pillow, bed sheets, one towel, one moth-eaten blanket, and the lumpy mattress. It took her three seconds to see I wasn't absconding with any such valuables, so I tipped her ten dollars for being so nice to me. She thanked me and said good-bye.

My suitcase was now even heavier than when I had arrived, so I took a shortcut through a field to Indian House. Nobody was back from working breakfast yet, so I sat down on some pebbles and unloaded a few of my books. I was still reading *Moby-Dick,* so I kept that one, but I left *Crime and Punishment, The Last of the Mohicans, Sexual Dysfunction, Genius Through the Ages,*

The Rise and Fall of Philosophy, and *Ship of Fools* for Mahatma to enjoy. The latter four I left on the basis of pure weight considerations rather than literary merit. I piled them up at the front door and left a note for Mahatma. Here is the text:

Dear Mahatma,

By now you probably know I was fired, but they probably didn't give you the specifics. It was because I refused to serve an elephant emetic. I never thought I'd make it so close to the end of the season and get discharged over an elephant emetic. Destiny is very strange. I want to thank you and Buddhakariskaman and Buddhafatima and all your fine Indian comrades. You were my best friends. I would love to write to you and have you write back. My address is Eugene Dingman, 93 Morton Street, Bayonne, New Jersey, Zip 07002. Much appreciation for introducing me to Shiva. Please write soon. If you're ever in Bayonne I'd like you all to meet my mother. If I'm in Detroit I'd love to see an assembly line. Again, my sincerest thanks and best wishes to your wives.

Cordially yours,
Eugene Dingman

After Indian House, I walked over the bridge and went to the bank. I told them I was closing my account, which totaled one thousand sixty-seven dollars and three cents including interest. They advised me on the pros and cons of traveling with that much money and taught me all about cashier's checks, American Express Travelers Checks, certified checks, money orders, and personal checking access, as well as the wisdom of leaving it with them in a time deposit certificate or IRA. They talked to me so much I realized I didn't

173

trust them, so I took the money in ten hundred-dollar bills, two twenties, two tens, one five, two singles and three cents. Then I took my suitcase and went into Hairy Mary's Place, ordered a diet cola, went into the men's room and put the ten hundreds in my left sock. The rest I kept in my right pocket like a normal person.

Then I came out and took a sip of my drink and went to the P.O. That's when I got the letter from my mother and three late copies of the *Bayonne News & Sun*. The P.O. is also the Loudon's Landing bus depot, so I checked the schedule and found out the sole daily bus comes through at 3:56 P.M. I didn't know what to do and I was really in a disintegrated, depressed state, so I sat down on a bench in front where the bus stops. After reading my mother's letter I was very glad I had some provocative reading material. Three stories were of particular interest to me:

A) CHICAGO LIBRARAN KIDNAPPED BY UFO
B) WIFE SHOOTS HUBBY AND BURIES HIM IN POTTED PLANTS
C) NUN BATTLES KILLER ANTS TO SAVE RADAR INSTALLATION

I crossed to the grocery store, bought a Clark bar, went back to the bench to read more of *Moby-Dick*. I got to the part where it was clear Ahab is the captain of a ship and wants to get even with a white whale who ate his leg. I was moved when Ahab says, ''Aye, it was Moby Dick that demasted me; Moby Dick that brought me to this dead stump I stand on now. Aye, aye! and I'll chase him round perdition's flames before I give him up!''

In fact, it was exactly then I realized I had so much

time before the bus that I could easily go for an hour's canoe ride.

Now I didn't realize any of this like a sane person. I was subconsciously completely crazy on the bus bench, and I guess I'd better record the missing parts that had pushed me over the edge. This was a last straw that had reduced me to an untouchable. In a month or two I'll be able to record more objectively about it, but where and when I'm writing this now forbids it. Actually, I'll simply list the missing facts so I can't be accused of slobbering in my soup. The missing parts are:

1) On my way to the dormitory after I was fired I saw a maroon Chrysler New Yorker pulling away from the porch and heading back down the employees' road toward the bridge.

2) I saw who was driving and who was sitting next to him and I ran at a right angle toward the moving vehicle.

3) The driver was my father.

4) He was less then three hundred feet away.

5) He saw me.

6) Laurette saw me.

7) They made believe they didn't see me.

8) My father speeded up the car and put his electric window up.

9) In a few seconds they were going too fast for me to catch them.

10) They left me in the dust.

11) They were gone.

That's when I turned around and continued on and went to the dorm to pack. I felt like my insides had been ripped out. Then Mrs. Brady gave me the package and note. Text as follows:

Dear Eugene,

Sorry we missed you. Your father hoped to have a talk with you about your letter. He hopes you like the Willowcross. It is the best brand in radios. Your father had one as a boy and used to listen to the police frequency and Singapore. Really sorry we will now have to wait until the fall to get together in NoHo. We're so excited about England. Enjoy the Willowcross.

Laurette and Dad

I have nothing more to say about that whole matter, Dear Diary, and so now I can just move on to Buzz-Ro-All and everything that happened all the way to the end.

The personnel at Buzz-Ro-All had been very nice to me all summer, and I rented one of the lockers in their cabana section to dig my swimming trunks, a terry-cloth shirt and No. 15 sun-block oil out of my suitcase. Then I locked my shoes, socks and money up for twenty-five cents and Buzz let me leave my suitcase behind the cash register and fish lures counter where they could keep an eye on it.

Before I even got into the canoe I knew Bunker was out on the lake, because I could see and hear him. There was no mystery about that. He was spraying with the airboat to the north in Blue Mountain Bay. From the end of the dock I could see him at a great distance, framed by the cement rectangle of the bridge. I really wasn't conscious of going on any kind of suicide mission or anything like that. All I knew was I felt like a despicable insect.

My mind really wasn't working right. I had the distinct impression I had been blasted with a shotgun and the BB's were sticking out all over my body. I knew it was the morning break time and so Della and everyone was on the loose. Particularly I wondered how much of my disgrace she knew about. She had to know I'd been fired. I decided she probably had had a big laugh when she heard. A big laugh and an awesome sigh of relief.

I paddled slowly out to go around the south tip of the island, the same way I had first gone with Della. I felt so different. Now I was not in a kaleidoscope. I was in a sanitarium. A terrarium. A mental submarine. I was compulsively pulling on my paddle as hard as I could and pointing the bow so it would hit the biggest waves and slap down with hard thuds so I felt like I was spanking myself. I paddled against a strong, crackling wind until I was exhausted. I called myself every ugly word I could think of. A few of them were: 1) Snooks, 2) Fruit, 3) Atheist, 4) Della Hater, 5) Alfredo Hater, 6) Weakling, 7) Sucker, 8) Complete Waste, 9) Naive Person, 10) Eye-Hand-Coordination Failure, 11) Idiot, 12) Sickie, 13) Reprobate, 14) Future Male Mouse, 15) Dope. My future did not look promising. There was a great deal I'd have to do to love myself, that much I suspected.

Finally my self-deprecation got so intense I got bored with it and started looking around at the beautiful lake. I knew this was the last I'd be seeing of Lake Henry and the hotel, and that sentiment began to calm me. If I knew a mantra I would have started chanting. The only thing I happened to remember was an ironic Shakespeare quote: "A star danced and under that was I born." I started chanting that over and over. It was very soothing even though it quite obviously had nothing to do with me.

I decided to let myself simply drift off the shore of the hotel. The wind quietly shifted, and now was coming from the south. I had several distinct thoughts, none of which connected to the other. Here are the ones I can remember:

A) Time is the real hero of life.

B) A diary can only lead to the grave.

C) I am waxing and waning.

D) Nobody is playing big chords on a pipe organ inside me.

E) Nobody ever really understands anyone else.

F) When *Homo sapiens* fall in love they try to get something and not give anything.

G) Laurette is a possessive, strictured person.

H) I hope Penelope finds happiness.

I) Nothing is constant.

J) Calvin Kennedy is a very disturbed person.

K) My mother is a very disturbed person.

L) What is Nancy Reagan really like? I think I like her.

M) Will the perfect person ever come along for me?

N) Am I best suited to be a CPA?

O) Will a Mafia leader ever manage to become elected President of the United States?

P) Is Della's mother mentally stable?

Q) How much would the laxative table have tipped?

R) All strong emotions bring with them the illusion of permanence.

S) Love is blind.

T) Is being alive the greatest adventure of them all?

U) Why do novelists always end books with deaths or marriages?

V) Am I returning to the scene of my crime?

I must have had a few dozen other intellectual thoughts, but these are all I can remember just now. Besides, by this time I had drifted up between the two islands at a point off the employees' dock. I was quite aware of the sound of Bunker's airboat. It wasn't terribly nearby, I figured. I could only hear the thing, but I decided to play it safe and really paddle very slowly just a few feet off the closest island. I still had a good look at the dock though, and a lot of the employees were swimming and sunbathing. I didn't really care. I didn't even care if they saw me swamped again. Big deal. Airboat swamps canoe. Newton figured out all the laws concerning that kind of stuff centuries ago.

As I really focused in on the specifics of the employees' dock I did get a little freaked out. There were really twice as many employees as usual, like they were having a sentimental swim-and-soak-up-the-rays salon now that the hotel would soon be shut and they'd all be off on their separate ways. There were the usual, including Captain Pegeen, Lola, three broiler chefs, the salad man, Scotty, almost the whole bellboy staff, three fourths of the waiters and waitresses, the beautician, a desk clerk, two valets, a section of chambermaids, Mrs. Brady, Louie, Huey, Mahatma and most of his gang on the grass ridge at the top of the stairs.

And Della.

I think they were all talking about me for three minutes, but then got bored and went ahead with their Australian crawls, sun reflectors, and private conversations. Della even turned completely to the side to really broadcast she was involved in a dialogue with Zola with her half-inch brow. The only one who simply rose above them all was Mahatma. He stood up and kept looking across the channel at me. He didn't wave or anything and neither did I.

Time was really running out. The bus would be coming. I had to get the canoe back. I decided to just cut across the channel toward the hotel island. Then I figured I'd hug that shoreline past the employees' dock and make it back without incident. I hadn't heard Bunker's boat for a while now, so I figured he was far away. I paddled out to the middle of the channel before I realized everyone was now looking at me, *and* something at the northern tip of the outer island. A lot of the employees were laughing, and when I looked behind me I saw Bunker was just drifting in the airboat and had been waiting all along for me to leave the shoreline. He started the airboat's engine with a roar. I began to paddle faster but I didn't want to show panic. This time for some reason I started humming the theme to the *Warsaw Concerto*. I couldn't figure out why until I remembered it was the background music from a movie called *Suicide Squadron*.

Bunker headed toward me, but he didn't have enough distance to get the airboat up to top speed. He turned north in a big circle.

I knew I'd never be able to make it to the hotel shore before he reached attack speed. I did the best I could, but in no time Bunker had the airboat barreling down the channel, roaring straight for my back. I didn't care about being swamped as long as I lived. And I was far past embarrassment as far as anyone watching was con-

180

cerned. Except one person. I realized I felt badly that Mahatma would see me wiped out. I turned to look at him high on the hill. His eyes were glued on me as I knew they would be. I wanted to shout, *I'm sorry*. I wanted to just yell and let him know I was helpless and not to worry about me because I didn't mind getting tossed in the lake again.

But then he did it.

Mahatma did it.

He made one of his circles in the air with his right hand.

He did it calmly, and something in the middle of my brain understood. I knew what the answer was, what I had to do.

I stopped paddling forward and suddenly planted my paddle deep and reversed my thrust.

In a second I had swung my canoe around and now I was paddling straight *toward* the closing airboat. It was an explosion of spray and violent winds heading straight at me with Bunker flying, his eyes popped out in shock. He couldn't believe I had reversed my direction and was now charging him. He had to turn the airboat suddenly because I was ready to jump out of the canoe and have it fly straight into his face.

His boat listed out of control as he flew by off to my right side. Its wake still came at me, but I just turned the canoe straight into it so I rode over the wave like a surfboard.

I was safe.

But Bunker was a different story.

He had to turn so sharply the airboat flipped, its motor boiling in the lake. Bunker was clear of the wreck, swimming for the dock.

The airboat sank.

Forgive me, God, but I was extraordinarily happy.

I gave Mahatma a tremendously jubilant wave and paddled my way back to Buzz-Ro-All. I also decided I would send him the Willowcross radio.

By 3:12 P.M. I was at the stop waiting with my suitcase and money back in my sock. I thought maybe Bunker would show up with a bazooka, but he didn't. I read my newspapers some more:

A) MARILYN MONROE'S GHOST APPEARS AT HYANNIS SUPERMARKET

B) PSYCHIC THREATENS TO TURN WIFE INTO FISH

C) DWARF-THROWING CONTEST CANCELED IN BONN

Employees on their afternoon break started arriving in town. Captain Pegeen walked right by and didn't say a word. One of the payola waiters gave me a tentative wave from across the street. That was about all the major action until I saw Della. She surprised me by coming slowly over to me.

"Hello," she said, sitting next to me.

"Hello," I said, in terrible pain.

"Bunker's all right," she mumbled. "He and the broiler guys are raising the airboat, but he's going to have to take the whole engine apart or it'll rust, you know."

I didn't say anything.

"You going back to Bayonne?" she asked, checking out my suitcase.

"Yes."

We sat there for a long while. I finally had to speak, because I felt she really wanted to express something but I didn't know what.

"Are you sure you don't love me?" I asked. I just couldn't bear the silence any longer.

"I don't."

"I just wanted to make sure you don't at least have a potential to love me in the future."

"I don't."

"You sure?" I felt so alone I would have said anything. Even auditory rejection seemed better than nothing.

"Absolutely."

"Then you don't feel about me like I feel about you."

"Oh, Eugene, there's so much you don't know about me."

"Like what?"

"Like I don't plan to ever get married to anyone. I think it's a very bourgeois institution that would put me in an inferior position. It's really passé. If only you'd have taken the time to truly get to understand and explore me, you'd know these nuances."

"You don't think you're ever going to marry anyone?" I asked.

"I do plan to have one close male confidant one day, but I'd always want us to have separate . . ."

"Bedrooms?" I offered.

"Apartments," she corrected.

"Oh."

"Eugene, don't you see you're a little too traditional for me?"

"I'm not traditional."

"Yes, you are. I plan to have a lot of experimental love affairs all my life just like my aunt Claire. Of course, my one special male friend I'd want to see at least once a day for camaraderie, but that's it."

"But won't you ever want children?"

"I'd never marry to have one," she said, as though I was really stupid. "Maternity is a bondage," she added.

"I understand." I nodded.

She craned her neck to look up the street. I could tell she was praying my bus was in sight. It wasn't.

"Do you have a religion?" I asked.

"I'm an atheist," she said, starting to play with the split ends of her hair.

"Aunt Claire, too?"

"Yes. Aunt Claire's really given me the courage to strive for freedom."

"She certainly has."

"She's taught me to detest accepted ideas and conformity."

"And you think you'll be happy?" I wanted to know. "How will you earn money?"

"I already told you."

"But how will you live?"

"I'm going to end up in France. Perhaps in the Saint-Germain-des-Prés district. You know how I feel about the French."

"Yes, I do," I said.

"Oh, Eugene, let's just stop this. Listen, you're a nice boy, but that's all you are at the moment. I wouldn't find it terribly painful to see you if I did travel near Bayonne. And if you happened to be skiing at Lake Placid or ice fishing and passed by Loudon's Landing you could call me and stop over. There'd be nothing wrong with that. We could go ice-skating. But I've got other things to do. Speaking French happens to be the most important thing in my life at the moment, but I don't expect you to believe that."

"What would you do if I didn't get on the bus now and just moved into the Pine Knoll Motel or rented a room and lived here for the rest of my life just to be near you?"

"I'd say you were out of your mind, Eugene. Let's at least say farewell with some kind of dignity."

"I want you to remember me as sensitive."

"Do you really mean that?" she wanted to know.

"Yes, I do."

"Then I will."

"But what's the last thing I can say to you? What's the normal thing I should do and say?"

"You don't know?"

"No. I could write it, but I'd have to think about it a very long time."

"You say *good-bye*."

"That's all?"

"Yes. You give me a kiss on the cheek and say good-bye."

"Good-bye."

"Good-bye."

Della got up, walked slowly away and disappeared up Hear Ye Road. I sat back on the bus-stop bench and made my final diary entries:

1) A) PSYCHIC VISIONS INFLUENCED MADAME CURIE

   B) MOM RESCUES KIDS FROM ALLIGATOR JAWS

   C) SCIENTISTS FIND WRECKAGE OF ANCIENT STARSHIP

2) "In the midst of winter I finally learned that there was in me an invincible summer."—Albert Camus

3) Eugene Dingman born.

The Awesome Truth
Paul Zindel

If you enjoyed reading Eugene's amazing and death-defying diary, you won't want to miss Paul Zindel's other characters and their antics. Their stories are thought-provoking, zany, and unique, but all of these books have one thing in common: they speak the awesome truth.

Confessions of a Teenage Baboon

"What I'm saying is that maybe the reason I'm so demanding of you is because you remind me of *me* when I was your age. Half developed. Half conscious. And half a man." He really glared at me now. "And that means you only have half your work done. Take a look at me. I'm twice your age and where has it gotten me? My life is no better than it was when I was fifteen. And kid, I don't want to see you make the same mistakes I did," he said, almost meekly. "I know what it's like to have a witch for a mother. And just because my father was around physically doesn't mean I had a father any more than you do. I really feel for you, kid, and I don't want to see you grow up twisted.''

"Is this what you brought me out here for? Is it?'' I asked. I hated myself for beginning to shake and lose my composure.

"Yes,'' he said matter-of-factly. I couldn't move. Finally I turned and started walking away, back toward the exit. I stopped in my tracks when Lloyd banged his foot on the roof of the car. It sounded like a shot. In a chilling whisper, he said, "One of these days your dead father will let go of you, and you'll be free. No more a slave to a dream which can never come true. Then, kid, it's up to you. You can cut the power line your mother has plugged into you, and stop blaming her for your failures. Start accepting the responsibility for your own life and then you can be a man.''

I turned to him and cried out: "What do you know about being a man!'' I felt an urge to really sock him one.

Lloyd flexed his muscles. "Look. I joined a gym. I put inches on my arm. I brought my voice down an octave! I even put a mirror in front of the telephone so I could study my expressions. I did everything I could to present myself as a man.'' Then he roared, banging his foot on the roof of the car again. *"Lloyd, the toughest man in town! 'King of the Kids!' Lloyd the Great still looking for Pop-Goes-the-Hero*. The outside looked *terrific,* but inside—forget it. What I didn't know was the change had to come from the inside first. I started the wrong way.''

The Girl Who Wanted a Boy

That's what she wanted, just to be able to sit with a boy and talk. But it would have to be a boy she felt something for. Someone who when she looked at him would make her think only how much she loved him. Love would be waiting for her somewhere, and she knew when she saw *that* boy, she would know it. When she saw the boy meant for her, there would be a circus in her heart—no, in her mind. It would be a mind circus. *Somewhere there was a boy who would give her a mind circus.*

There was something about this boy that was leaping out of the newspaper, machine-gunning Sibella Cametta from the sports page of the *Staten Island Advance*. A machine gun screaming, *"I am fun and romance."*

"What's the matter, Sibella?" she heard her mother say.

"Oh, nothing," Sibella said. She was fighting a distinct desire to lift the sports page up to her lips and start kissing the photo of this unknown mechanic. She wanted to dive into the newspaper. She wanted to cut the picture out, tear it out, and wear it on her heart. Mariner's Midgets became a poem.

"Excuse me, Mother," Sibella said. "I have a little indigestion. I'm going to need an Alka-Seltzer."

"Of course, dear," Mrs. Cametta agreed.

"Gas is really terrible," Charlie sympathized.

Sibella got up gently from the table.

"Are you finished with the newspaper?" she asked.

"Oh, sure," Charlie said.

"Thank you." Sibella picked up the paper as though it was a priceless Dead Sea Scroll. She tried not to appear excited as she moved out of the dining room and started up the stairs. As she neared her room she picked up speed. She flung the door open, slammed it shut, leaped across the bed, and spread the picture out again. She ripped her diary off the bookcase, and she began to write frantically and passionately, "Dear Diary, On this day I have found *the boy*."

Harry and Hortense at Hormone High

"You said last night that you had a story about a hero?" I shot at him, because this was what we really cared about, or at least I did.

"Oh, yes," Jason said, his eyes lighting up. "I need you to write a story about a hero who is greater than any astronaut, any president, greater than Alexander the Great, or anyone you could possibly think of!"

"Oh?" I said.

"A hero has come at last to save the world," Jason went on, "but he needs you to help tell everybody before it's too late!"

"Who is this hero?" Hortense asked, putting down the glass of papaya juice Jason had thrust into her hand.

"Me," Jason said.

"Tell us more," Hortense urged.

Jason relaxed.

"Back in places like ancient Greece there came a

time when nobody was working together. Everybody was split apart. Two thousand years ago there was no sense of unity, just like now! Look at our high school! It's worse than the labyrinth needed to hold the Minotaur monster. The hallways are the paths of the maze, and Dean Niboff is just one of the beasts leading the flesh eaters to devour new batches of youths term after term!''

"But what does that have to do with you?" Hortense asked.

"It has to do with my *job*."

"What job?" I asked.

"Well, I'm embarrassed to say this because I can sense you're uncomfortable with me," he said.

"*Please* tell us," Hortense urged, and just then Darwin came running into the room, plopped down, and rested his head on Jason's foot. The dog looked at us with its big mournful eyes.

Jason began to speak more hesitantly, carefully.

"Well, you see, I think it's my purpose to lead everyone out of the dark labyrinth." He petted Darwin's huge head gently.

"You're here to lead us out?" Hortense repeated.

I Never Loved Your Mind

I walked along with her, even though she'd started making terrible sounds under her breath.

"I just wanted to be friends," I advised.

"Pick on somebody else."

"Don't you want me to walk you home?"

"No!"

"They say if any two people are exposed to each other long enough, they begin to like each other."

She fumed. "I don't want you exposed to me."

I began whistling. Then my left cheek began to twitch.

"I'm sorry for coming on so strong last week."

"*Ummmm.*"

"I am."

I noticed a lessening of the shade of scarlet in her left eye, so I let her digest the apology as we crossed a busy intersection. A car headed for us, and I gave her arm an assist. She shook it loose like a muskrat freeing its leg from a trap.

"Like me to carry the shopping bag?"

She didn't answer.

"It looks so *heavy.*"

She still didn't answer.

"Don't you have *friends?*" she asked.

That afternoon I spent my break in the autopsy room. I guess I knew all along I was going to write a letter:

Dear Yvette:

I'm leaving work five minutes early today, so by the time you find this in your shopping bag I'll be gone and you can read it without anxiety. Even save it until you get home, but the important thing is that you read it. You're probably saying to yourself "Why me?" again. Well, I have a feeling about you. I have a feeling you're a very special individual. I have a vision that in some weird and bizarre way you and I have a destiny with each other. Could we go out Friday night? Please

answer me. I'm going to send you flowers or candy
every day until you do. Let's be friends, Yvette, before
it's too late..

> Sincerely yours,
> Dewey Daniels

My Darling, My Hamburger

"You like swimming?" Maggie asked.

"It's all right," Dennis replied. "Do you like it?"

"It's nice in the summer."

"It's too cold now."

"Yeah."

"Where do you go swimming when it's warm enough?" Maggie pursued.

"Down here—or else Wolf's Pond. Lot of rocks there."

"I heard that."

"It's true."

Maggie noticed his left hand getting closer every minute, and his fingers were tapping like a pneumatic drill. She felt as though it were a spider getting ready to drop on her shoulder.

"I was here the day Mel Haughting drowned."

"Really?" Maggie was interested. Mel Haughting had been in her chemistry class.

"They were stoned and were out on a raft over *that* way." Dennis pointed. "He got stuck under it, and nobody noticed until it was too late."

She looked impressed, he thought. Maybe he ought to try kissing her. Make his move just for the heck of

t. Chalk it up to experience. Liz and Sean wouldn't be back for a little while, and even if she slapped him, it wouldn't matter.

He moved closer. She pretended to be looking in the other direction. He turned her head toward him. His lips touched hers. Almost. The kiss was on the left side of her mouth, but with a little wiggle everything lined up all right.

He kept his lips pressed against hers for a few moments, and he was surprised she didn't pull away. *"She's letting me kiss her,"* he told himself. *"She's letting me kiss her."* In the middle of the kiss he opened his eyes, and he almost jumped. She was looking right back at him!

"I th . . . th . . . th . . . think," she stuttered. "I think we'd better go get a hamburger."

Pardon Me, You're Stepping on My Eyeball!

All Miss Edna Shinglebox ever did was keep her mouth shut and nod and be boring and try to agree with everybody. No more." Edna said to herself, wanting to shake her finger at the girl in the mirror. "Oh, yes, you're lonely all right, and you need friends, but you've got to do something to earn them. Edna Shinglebox, you're a yes-woman, that's what you are! All you do is say 'yes.' Kids who say nothing but yes all the time don't have any backbone. Edna Shinglebox, you're a jellyfish."

Edna's mind was racing on. Everything was getting

clearer and clearer for her now. It was as though things were suddenly beginning to fall into place now that she was believing in her own thoughts. It seemed like there was a voice inside of her that was growing stronger and stronger, and that voice belonged to whoever the real Edna Shinglebox was going to be. And that voice was saying. "Marsh Mellow, you are the world's biggest liar. You think I don't know that's your handwriting in those letters? You think I don't notice the handwriting in your notebook is the same as in those letters? You think I didn't notice the way you phonied up the postage stamp on the envelope and with that return address to a nuthouse called the Los Angeles Neurological Hospital for the Insane and Crazy? You must think I'm an idiot! I don't fall for your gibberish about your father who hasn't written, and is locked in solitary confinement waiting for a lobotomy. Those kinds of crazy ideas are fiction! Those letters read just like you talk, Mr. Marsh Mellow. And let me tell you one thing, Edna Shinglebox may look dumb, but she's not dumb anymore. The big plot . . . the eucalyptus tree . . . they're going to operate on your father's brain, my foot! You're the one that's freaked out, buster, and when I see you, you're going to get yours, that much I can promise you!"

The Pigman

Mr. Pignati and I went into the room with all the pigs, and I started lifting the bigger ones to see what country they were made in.

You could hear Lorraine upstairs for about five minutes. When she same downstairs, she had this picture in her hands.

"Who's this?"

There was a pause. Then the smile faded off the Pigman's face. He took the picture from her and moved over to the stuffed armchair and sat down.

"My wife Conchetta," he said, "in her confirmation dress."

"Conchetta?" Lorraine repeated nervously. We both knew something was wrong but couldn't put our finger on it. I got the idea that maybe his wife had run off to California and left him. I mean, you couldn't blame her when you stop to think that her husband's idea of a big time was to go to the zoo and feed a baboon.

"She liked that picture because of the dress," he went on. "It was the only picture she ever liked of herself."

He got up and put it in the table drawer where all those old *Popular Mechanics* books were, and when he turned around, his eyes looked like he was going to start crying. Suddenly he forced a smile and said, "Go upstairs and look around while I get you some wine. Please feel at home, please. . . ."

* * *

The bedroom had a closet too, so I started with that. There were all kinds of dresses in it, and lacy ladies' coats, and hats that looked like they must have been the purple rage at the turn of the tenth century. It was a big loss; it really was. And let me tell you, this room was a little nerve-racking too. It had a double bed with a cover made of millions of ruffles, and the way the pillows were laid out, it looked like there might be a dead body underneath. I checked that out right away, but there were only pillows. Then I found one drawer in the dresser bureau that had a lot of papers in it.

Then I found this bill right in with all the jewelry and junk and her Social Security card, and that's when I knew Conchetta Pignati was not in California. I knew that where Conchetta Pignati was she was never coming back.

The Pigman's Legacy

"Mr. Pignati's spirit is here," John said. "I can feel it. I really can."

My throat felt as though it was going to close. The capillaries in my head were like the strings on a piano pounding out some atonal etude. It was all so unscientific, I wanted to say. We should get notes. We should have oscilloscopes. We should have electrodes in our heads. We should be recording all this for *Psychology Today* or some other illustrious scientific journal. Instead I said nothing and allowed John to haul me up alongside him. At the top of the stairs, we could see into the bathroom. Everything looked okay there.

"It's the same old shower curtain," John pointed out. I watched him go in and open the medicine cabinet. Some shaving cream was in there. And for some bizarre reason John's face lit up at that discovery. "Somone *is* here," he said with an assurance that made my jaw petrify.

"Let's get out of here," I finally managed to utter.

"Mr. Pignati, are you there?" John began to speak to the air in front of him. "It's John and Lorraine," John called gently into the hallway leading to the Pigman's old bedroom.

The door to the room was closed, but the scraping sound from beyond reached my ears with no trouble at all.

"Did you hear that?" I asked John.

"Naw," John said, "it's nothing."

"Are you crazy? It sounds like the top of a coffin sliding to the floor."

"Mr. Pignati," John called again, knocking gently on the door now.

And what happened next almost gave me a thrombosis.

"Come in," an old man's voice demanded.

John and I grabbed each other as though we had just been sentenced to death. We watched in terror as the owner of the voice from the other side started to open the door.

The Undertaker's Gone Bananas

"Hello?" came Lauri's voice on the phone.

Bobby hesitated speaking. Already he was sorry he had even dialed the number. He didn't want to mix her up in this but it was too late.

"Hello? Hello?" Lauri's voice repeated.

Bobby spoke. "I think he just knocked her off," he blurted.

"What?" Lauri asked. "Bobby, is that you?"

"Yes," Bobby said. "I think Hulka just knocked off his wife."

"Bobby, it's too early for a joke. Come on down and have some Special K."

"Lauri, I'm serious! Call the cops!"

"Bobby, I don't think this is very funny."

"Look, he might jump around the terrace any minute and come after me. I threw a chair over there."

"You threw a chair?"

"Lauri, have your mother call."

"Bobby, are you practicing a scene?"

Bobby practically gagged, so many words began to collect in this throat. "Lauri, you're the last one I want to have to think about this, but get somebody to call the cops. They won't believe me. Get the doorman, the super, anybody. Get them up here. I can't talk anymore. Just tell them and then make believe I didn't call and go back to sleep."

"Are you *sure?*" Lauri asked.

"Just call," Bobby ordered. "I've got to get over there and check it out."

"Don't!" Lauri screamed into the receiver as Bobby hung up.